Praise for Laura Crum's *Going, Gone*

"In her eleventh outing, veterinarian Gail McCarthy and her family go on a horse camping trip to a ranch owned by her old boyfriend.... VERDICT: Bringing back Lonny and Bret in this long-running series is just what fans wanted. A good murder mystery that packs quite a wallop."

—*Library Journal*

"The relationship between Gail and her son, and how to answer questions about death and what happens afterwards occupy center stage. Crum saves the main action for an exciting climax."

—*Gumshoe Review*

"Crum has a real talent for painting beautiful backdrops for her novels, with the wide open expanses of the Sierra Nevada foothills in *Going, Gone* being no exception. She can also craft thrilling action scenes, including a heart-stopping one that comes near the end of this book."

—*Hidden Staircase*

"I'm an unabashed fan of Laura Crum's mysteries.... She makes [catching the murderer in *Going, Gone*] a most suspenseful and intriguing process, so there's nothing ho-hum about this adventure.... This is a fast-moving thriller that you won't want to put down once you're into it."

—*The Columnists.com*

"Crum's solid knowledge of horses and the ranching life will appeal to horse-loving mystery fans...."

—*Publishers Weekly*

D1530863

Barnstorming

A Gail McCarthy Mystery

*B*arnstorming

A Gail McCarthy Mystery

Laura Crum

2012
PERSEVERANCE PRESS/JOHN DANIEL & COMPANY
PALO ALTO/MCKINLEYVILLE, CALIFORNIA

A Perseverance Press Book
Published by John Daniel & Company
A division of Daniel & Daniel, Publishers, Inc.
Post Office Box 2790
McKinleyville, California 95519
www.danielpublishing.com/perseverance

Distributed by SCB Distributors (800) 729-6423

Book design by Eric Larson, Studio E Books, Santa Barbara
Cover design and illustration by Peter Thorpe

10 9 8 7 6 5 4 3 2 1

LIBRARY OF CONGRESS CATALOGING-IN-PUBLICATION DATA
Crum, Laura.
  Barnstorming : a Gail McCarthy mystery / by Laura Crum.
    p. cm.
  ISBN 978-1-56474-508-8 (pbk. : alk. paper)
  1. McCarthy, Gail (Fictitious character)—Fiction. 2. Santa Cruz County (Calif.)—
Fiction. I. Title.
  PS3553.R76B37 2012
  813'.54—dc23
              2011034308

For Andy and Zak,
with all my love

— . —

Many thanks to Henry and Sunny,
our partners in exploring the
trails along the ridge

Author's Note

THIS BOOK is the twelfth in my series featuring equine veterinarian Gail McCarthy. I began the series in 1994, with *Cutter*, and with the intent of completing a dozen books. Gail is thirty-one years of age in the first book—I was in my early thirties when I wrote it. She ages one year per book in the first ten books. In book number eleven, *Going, Gone*, she has aged five years since the previous book, *Chasing Cans*. And again, in this book, *Barnstorming*, another five years have passed since *Going, Gone*. Gail has just reached her fiftieth birthday.

There were several reasons behind my choice to jump five years in the last two books. I wanted to catch Gail up to my own age more or less—I'm in my early fifties now. And I wanted to write about a theme which fits better with one's fifties than earlier in life. Also, I wanted to show the growth of Gail's son in four very different stages. *Moonblind* deals with the challenges of pregnancy, *Chasing Cans* with the delights and dismays of a nursing baby, and *Going, Gone* with the wonder of a small child. In this book, Mac is eleven and moving forward toward adolescence.

Many people have asked if Gail is "me" (others just assume it). The answer is mixed. I was never a vet, I never placed the priority on career and work that Gail did, I did not spend a large part of my adult life as a single woman. Unlike Gail, I did spend a big part of my life training and showing cowhorses of various sorts. However, Gail and I share many similar opinions and I have given Gail my own horses for hers, as well as my dogs and cats and other animals. Her home is based on my home and her husband and son bear a great resemblance to my husband and son. In many ways these books are a lovesong to my own life and the things that have delighted me—my family, animals, home, garden, the land where I live…etc. If I have made any of it come alive and shown how lovely it all is, then I am grateful.

Since these stories are mysteries, there must be a central crime on which the plot turns. Unlike the background of the books, the crimes have sprung from my imagination, but every single one is based (often loosely) on some true story I have heard or known about, and I have tried to keep them all within the bounds of what might be possible. A friend once told me that for my books to become "successful," I needed to write characters and stories that were "bigger than life." I'm afraid that doesn't interest me. Life interests me, and I have tried to write stories that were/are faithful to life as I've known it.

Ever since *Hayburner* (my seventh book), I've received plenty of email asking if the current book is the last one. There's a reason for this. The series seemed to me to be on shaky ground, as it has never been hugely successful, and I wrote the books such that if each one after *Hayburner* were the last, it would seem a fitting conclusion. However, I have been fortunate enough to continue to be published and I would like to thank both St. Martin's Press, my first publisher, and Perseverance Press, my current publisher, for that privilege. And so, here I am, having reached my initial goal of a dozen books.

Will this book be the last? Probably. I know enough to know that I don't know, if you see what I mean. I promise not to push Gail off any cliffs, if you're just getting ready to read the book. But perhaps her future is best left to the imagination. We'll see.

Barnstorming

Chapter 1

I WAS RIDING MY PALOMINO gelding along the ridge, my eyes on the shafts of afternoon sunlight slanting between the eucalyptus trees, my mind elsewhere. Pondering what I wanted to do with the rest of my life, actually. So it was Sunny who spotted the white mare. His yellow ears pricked sharply forward, his head came up a couple of inches, and he checked. I looked where he was looking and saw the horse and rider.

Jane Kelly and her Arab mare were coming down the ridge trail, headed in our direction. I knew Jane and her mount from way back, from over ten years ago when I had been a practicing equine veterinarian. Then, Jane had been one of my clients. Lately I'd been meeting her from time to time out on the trails. Jane was always by herself, riding Dolly, whose dapple gray color had gone white with age. I was usually with my son, Mac, on his steady sorrel gelding, Henry. But Henry had colicked three months ago, and we had sent him to colic surgery to save his life. While Henry was recovering, my trail rides were solo, too.

I pulled Sunny up and said, "Hi Jane," wanting to warn both her and her horse that I was ahead of her. Some horses could spook quite violently when startled by an unexpected horse and rider.

Not Dolly. She lifted her head at my voice and the sight of Sunny, but didn't vary her steady pace. Which was perhaps not unexpected. Dolly had to be about twenty years old, and had been a trail horse for most of that time.

Jane looked up at the sound of my voice and then halted her horse about fifteen feet from me. She smiled. "Well, Gail McCarthy," she said. "How are you doing these days?"

"Just fine," I said, "and you?" I was not about to bore Jane with my current predicament; she was at best a casual acquaintance.

Jane shrugged. "I just moved Dolly to Lazy Valley Stable. I'm sick of that bitch at the Red Barn."

I knew which bitch she meant. Tammi Martinez currently ran the Red Barn and she had not endeared herself to many of the boarders. On the other hand, feisty Jane had left a good many previous boarding stables in an irate tizzy. Jane wasn't easy to get along with either.

"Didn't you used to board at Lazy Valley before?" I asked.

"Yeah." Jane shrugged again. "I'm not nuts about them, either. They charge way too much, and Juli, the woman that owns it, spouts that natural horsemanship bullshit all the time. Drives me crazy. But at least they have decent access to the trails." Jane shot me a look. "Have you run into that guy with the big white dog? Bill Waters?"

"The guy who lives in that house down below here? Near the trail?" I asked.

"Yeah, him."

"He sicced that dog on me once," I said mildly.

Jane literally ground her teeth. "He just did that to me last week. The guy's an asshole. I called the sheriffs on him. We've got a right-of-way through there. He has no damn business doing that. He almost got this one girl killed when her horse bolted."

"Fortunately Sunny doesn't mind dogs," I said. "He ignored the stupid thing. So did my son's horse. But it wouldn't have been funny if the dog had spooked them."

"No," said Jane. "And the guy has no damn right to do it. The sheriff's deputy said to call them if he does it again."

"Is he the only trail access problem?" I was genuinely curious. I used the same trails that the boarding stable did. Trail access was an issue for me, too.

"Hell, no. You know that subdivision that went in?"

I nodded.

"Well, they won't let us ride through there, either, so that way is blocked."

"Uh-huh," I said. I knew about the subdivision and its un-horsey residents, who didn't care for equine hooves, or manure, on their pristine pavement. I also knew a little sidehill trail that detoured around the whole establishment and brought you out on the ridge. I decided to keep that knowledge to myself, for the moment.

"And the high school put up a frisbee golf course, so it's hard to ride through there now without getting nailed by a flying disc. Even Dolly doesn't care for that," Jane stroked her mare's white neck, "and she's a good girl."

"Yeah, I know," I said. "Sunny's a good boy, too, and I don't much care to ride through the high school anymore, either. Too many people and flying objects for my taste."

"So, it just leaves the ridge trail, which is steep, and some nasty neighbor, we don't know who, keeps trying to block it."

"I noticed that," I said. "I wondered what it was all about."

Barriers of downed trees and branches kept appearing across that trail. Some we could step over, others we detoured around, sometimes we had to retrace our steps.

"Some piece of crap is trying to keep horses off the trails." I could see Jane's jaw clench. "They've got no right."

"I wish they'd concentrate on keeping the dirt bikes off the trail," I said. "I ran into one the other day. Sunny was fine, and it went by us with no problem, but I kept wondering what would happen if I met one coming around a blind corner at a good speed. What if there was nowhere for me to get out of the way? Even Sunny is not gonna put up with a dirt bike sliding underneath him. And the worst thing about it was, this guy on the bike just ignored me, acted like I wasn't there."

"I know." Jane shook her head. "Those damn bikers are the worst. Did the guy have a big bushy beard?"

"Yeah, he did," I said slowly, "now that you mention it. Do you know him?"

"He's a jerk," Jane said fiercely. "I've met him out here myself. Racing around. He doesn't give a flying whatever if he spooks your horse. He's gonna get somebody killed. I flip him off whenever I see him."

I sighed. "I love being out on the trails," I said, in a slightly more heartfelt tone than I'd meant to use. It was the truth, though. "I worry that it will just get to be too stressful to get here."

"Me, too," Jane said, "which is why I moved back to Lazy Valley. They can ride right out their back gate onto the trails."

"Yeah, I know," I agreed. "I've ridden over there a few times. Why did you move Dolly to the Red Barn to begin with?"

I thought I knew the answer to this, but was curious to hear Jane's story.

"That bitch Sheryl Silverman stole my boyfriend," Jane snapped. Always frank, old Jane. "I didn't want to set eyes on either one of them again."

"But you don't mind anymore?"

"Well, actually, Doug and I are back together, so I guess I stole him back." Jane grinned. "I don't mind seeing Sheryl these days. She may not care to see me."

I laughed. I knew Sheryl Silverman. I might not have employed the same term that Jane had used, but my sentiments were similar. Sheryl was a nasty piece of work. But young and good-looking enough to get away with it. She kept her horse at Lazy Valley Stable, and spent her time flirting with the wannabe cowboys who hung around there.

Looking at the fine lines around Jane's blue eyes and the streaks of gray in her dark blond hair, I realized with a sense of shock that

I probably looked roughly similar. I had turned fifty this year; my hair, too, was gray-streaked, my wrinkles quite obvious, and I carried twenty pounds I didn't need.

"Good for you," I said with a grin.

Jane answered as if she could read my mind. "Oh, I may not be as cute as Sheryl—not anymore—but in the end, I think Doug got bored with her. She really doesn't have much to say."

Or much brain, I thought. Jane, on the other hand, was plenty sharp and had lots to say. The trouble was her feisty nature, which often rubbed people the wrong way. Jane never seemed to keep boyfriends long, or friends, for that matter. I'd gotten along with her well enough over the years, but we'd never been close. Not that I was prone to making many close friendships myself.

"The worst thing about Lazy Valley," Jane added, "is the damn owner. Juli and her boyfriend Jonah run the place, and they are so, so into that stupid natural horsemanship crap. It just makes me want to throw up."

I grinned. I knew the owner of Lazy Valley. Also her boyfriend, who was the resident trainer. Both of them were huge fans and students of one of the preeminent natural horsemanship gurus.

"Don't you hate that shit?" Jane asked me.

I shrugged. "I don't see much point in it."

"It's all people who don't know much about horses and are afraid to get on them and ride them." Jane sniffed. "They feel safer on the ground playing these games with the horse, and then they get to call themselves a trainer without ever learning to ride. The trouble is, the horses don't like it. It makes them cranky and uncooperative. And pushy. I've never seen one horse come out of these natural horsemanship programs that I thought much of."

"I know what you mean," I said mildly, not wanting to encourage Jane in another tirade.

Dolly rooted her nose a little and shifted her front feet, and Jane bumped her with the bit. "No, girl, we're not going home until I say so."

Sunny, I was pleased to note, was standing like a park bench. This was one of my little yellow horse's many desirable qualities. He would stand flat-footed and still whenever he was asked to, patiently waiting for me to get done with whatever I was up to.

Jane glanced at Sunny. "He seems like a pretty cool customer," she said.

"He is that," I agreed.

"Where did he come from? I remember you used to ride a big bay horse with a blaze and one blue eye, and a smaller light brown horse with a white star."

"Gunner and Plumber," I said, and smiled. "I still have them. Gunner's retired to pasture. He's doing well. Plumber is twenty-two. He's sound, but a little peggy. We still ride him, but he doesn't care much for hills. I use Sunny when I want to go out on the trails."

"Where did you get him?" Jane asked again.

"Up in the Sierra foothills," I answered. It was a long story, and one that I didn't feel like telling now. "I was told he came from Mexico via a horse trader. He's a good trail horse," I added.

Jane looked Sunny over. I knew what she was seeing. A small, thick-bodied critter, about 14.3 hands, Sunny looks like a Quarter Horse crossed on a large pony. He has big feet, like a draft horse, and is sturdily made, with plenty of bone and a slightly coarse look to him. But somehow, maybe it's the bright gold color, or the long white mane and tail, or the big brown eyes, or the white stripe running down an attractive (though not small) head, the main thing Sunny is, is cute. Little girls mobbed me when I rode by the boarding stable. Experienced horsemen grinned and stroked his neck. Sunny is just that cute. Not fancy, well-bred-horse cute. Little-girl-stuffed-toy-pony cute.

Jane smiled. I could hear it coming. "He's cute," she said.

"Yep," I agreed. "And a good trail horse."

"What more could you ask? I don't know what I'm going to do when Dolly gets too old to go out on the trails. We've been a team for so long." Jane stroked her mare's white neck. Dolly shifted her front feet restlessly. Jane looked over her shoulder. "Boy, there are a lot of people out on the trails today," she added. "I saw Ross Hart, that guy who trains horses at the Red Barn just a few minutes ago. If looks could kill, I'd be dead."

"Why's that?" I asked, even though I was not much interested in boarding stable gossip.

"Oh, he thinks he's a hot-shot trainer and I talked several of his clients out of working with him. I'm giving riding lessons myself these days; I've had a bit more experience than Ross. Besides, I don't care for him. He's been up to some stuff he shouldn't be up to." She sniffed. "I told him so."

Staring at Jane, I wondered what she was implying. I had once known a horse trainer who had a thriving business on the side selling cocaine. Young Ross Hart looked tough enough to fill that role. I changed the subject.

"I never see anyone out here when I ride on the weekdays," I said, "but on the weekends I usually run into at least one or two people."

Jane grinned. "Well, I've already met four different folks this afternoon." Her mare shifted her front feet again and Jane patted her neck. "Okay, Dolly." Jane smiled at me. "I'd better get going. Dolly's had enough of this visiting. Good to see you."

"Likewise," I said, and kicked Sunny forward.

Our two horses passed amiably in a wide spot in the trail and then I was marching up the ridge, Jane and her issues behind me.

At least Jane had distracted me from my own issues. For a while I just rode, watching the scenery, letting my mind drift.

The trail followed the ridgeline, running through a forest of eucalyptus trees, their peeling, pinkish trunks rising above me, creaking slightly in the breeze that rustled the long lance-like blue-green leaves far overhead. Afternoon sunlight shafted between them, barring and dappling the trail with golden autumn light.

It was early October and the patches of sky I could see were an intense deep violet blue, the air sparkled with a faint tingle, and the shady spots on the trail made me shiver. Sunny's coat had gone from sleek gold to a fuzzy buttermilk yellow. Fall was here.

Sunny marched along and we left the eucalyptus trees behind as the trail ascended into an open area studded with big Monterey pines. Passing on my left was the skeleton of the biggest one, a forked trunk that I could see from my porch, towering above the ridgeline. We called it the "landmark tree." Ahead of me the trail descended to a little flat where it joined another trail. This spot we called the "three-way trail crossing." Down below I could see the wide-open spaces of a pampas grass studded meadow, criss-crossed with motorcycle tracks; this was where the dirt bike riders hung out. I scanned it carefully but there was no noise and no motion. All quiet today.

Sunny and I reached the trail junction. Sunny's preference was to take the left-hand fork, which led toward home. But I reined him to the right, and, reluctantly, Sunny obeyed. Dragging his feet, he shuffled down a slight grade and through a tunnel of tangled berry vines, brambles, and brushy willows. Lemony splashes of sunlight spangled the deep shady dark earth of the trail. Then we were out of the shrubbery tunnel and climbing a steep hill.

I could both hear and feel the horse huffing as he trudged up the grade. He broke into a trot, using his momentum to help defeat the slope. Up we went, through live oaks and redwood trees, until we reached another little wide-open flat. And here Sunny paused, looking ahead, ears pricked sharply forward. I looked where he was looking.

Motion, coming through the trees, resolved itself into a sorrel horse with a flaxen mane and tail and a white blaze. The rider wore a cowboy hat and had a long blond braid. Despite my desire for peace and solitude, I had to smile. Sheryl Silverman was out riding the trails today. Given what I had just heard, this seemed a bit ironic.

I didn't care much for Sheryl; she fancied herself an expert on everything to do with horses, and her opinion of herself was vastly overrated, as far as I was concerned. However, Jane's story had amused me. The thought of Jane stealing her boyfriend back from Sheryl made me grin.

Sunny and I stood quietly on the flat. Sheryl and her sorrel mare rode toward us, but both seemed unaware of our presence. This was fine with me. If Sheryl took the trail that led up the hill to my right, she might never notice me at all. But horse and rider came on steadily, passing the trail that led to the Lookout, and I saw Sheryl's abstracted expression jerk into awareness as she spotted me; her eyes narrowed.

"Hi Sheryl," I said.

Sheryl pulled her horse up. "Hello, Gail, fancy meeting you here."

"I ride here quite a bit," I said, "though I don't often see anyone else. This must be my lucky day. First I met Jane Kelly and now you." And I smiled.

As I'd expected, the mention of Jane nettled Sheryl. She tossed her blond braid over her shoulder and gave her horse a sharp jerk in the mouth, apparently unconsciously. At the same time, she obviously had no idea what to say to me. Her mare danced and fretted, and a look of sheer rage crossed Sheryl's superficially pretty face. I suddenly wondered why I'd provoked her.

In her thirties, blond and tan and slim, with lots of makeup and silver jewelry and a brittle, tinkly laugh, Sheryl was everything I wasn't. She favored the party scene and went from one cowboy, or wannabe cowboy, to the next, with absolutely no scruples concerning their marital status. She spent most of her time hanging around the barn, flirting; I had never seen her out on a solo trail ride before. It amused me to note that she wore a fringed leather jacket and had matching saddlebags with an equal amount of fringe.

"What a nice afternoon," I said belatedly, "and I'd better get going," I added, "if I want to be home before dark."

This wasn't really true; I had plenty of time to get home before dark, even if I dawdled quite a bit. But I was sorry I had needled Sheryl, and I was also suddenly sure that I did not want to have a conversation with her.

"Have a good ride," I told her.

Still quite obviously annoyed, Sheryl jerked her chin at me in reply and rode past on her prancing mare.

I watched her heading down the trail in the same direction Jane had gone, and aimed Sunny up the hill to the Lookout.

This last piece of trail was steep, ascending sharply through the redwoods to emerge in a grove of big, old madrones, their red branches twisting sinuously as they reached for the deep blue sky far above. The trail threaded between them into a small flat at the very top of the bluff. I could see the dark blue velvety folds of the coastal hills rolling and tossing away in the distance on all sides, and before me, aquamarine in the bittersweet brilliance of the autumn sunshine, bright on the horizon, lay the blue curve of the Monterey Bay. Beyond that—I squinted at the dazzle of white light—the rim of the world and the westering sun.

I walked Sunny across the flat to the edge of the bluff and let him rest. I could feel his breath move my legs in and out as he got his wind back after the climb. We were both content to stand still.

Staring out at the view, seeing it and not seeing it. One part of me registered the familiar drama with an equally familiar appreciative thrill. I came here often and never tired of it. The other part of my mind had gone back to puzzling over my current predicament. The busy inward chatter was both welcome and unwelcome. I longed for my mind to be quiet and able simply to take in the beauty around me, and at the same time my problem obsessed me; I needed to chew on it as a dog needs to chew on a bone.

A red-tail hawk cut across the abyss of air before me, swimming through the sky level with my horse, as we stood at the edge of the Lookout bluff. Free as a bird, I thought distractedly. Free. And that was the point. Did I want to be free?

The hawk disappeared into the distance. I watched him go, saw him become a tiny dot and then vanish. Going, gone. Like all of us. Like life itself.

I sighed, and felt Sunny sigh underneath me. The horse cocked a hind leg, clearly prepared to rest awhile. Sunny knew me. He knew I wanted to sit here and think.

I had a choice to make. And after weeks and months of mulling it over, I still couldn't decide what I should do. Being free sounded simple; it even looked simple, watching a hawk soar across the sky. But in practice, not so simple.

For I now had what most people claim to want. Financial freedom. The choice of working or not working. I only needed to please myself. After ten years of steadily making a living as a horse vet, and another ten years of raising my child while my husband worked hard to support us, I found myself facing the oddest problem I had yet encountered. My husband had inherited an almond orchard when his father died. The almond orchard brought in over a hundred thousand a year, without either Blue or I needing to do much of anything. We were both free to work or not. Blue had promptly retired.

That was six months ago. In the ensuing time, Blue had built a small separate building to serve as an addition to our little house and taken up playing the bagpipes. He also tended his beloved vegetable garden and cooked dinner every evening. Blue was gloriously unconflicted, always busy, and quite happy. I was the one who was having problems.

After ten years of raising my child, the last few as a homeschooling mom, I was finding that eleven-year-old Mac needed me less and less. He now went to school a couple of days a week, was able to be home alone, and had Blue for support when needed. I was free, in every way, to resume my interrupted career as a horse vet. And this career had meant a lot to me. I'd always intended to go back to it. I remained a partner in the veterinary firm.

Free, free, free. I shook my head in aggravation, like a woman being plagued by gnats. I was free to work if I wanted to. And I was free not to work.

And do what, a friend of mine had asked.

That was the point, exactly. The wind blew a strand of my hair across my face. I brushed it away, and reached down to smooth Sunny's cream-colored mane back in place on his neck. The freedom that I sometimes envisioned didn't look like doing anything much. It wasn't something that I could defend or explain. I only knew it drew me, as the wind and the hawk and the distance drew me. But could I stand it?

All my life's training had been to be busy, productive, independent. Even as a mother, giving up my career to stay home with my child, I had felt confident in the importance of what I was doing, affirmed in my belief that nurturing one's child was a valid choice. Perhaps not glamorous, but nonetheless, realistically, important work.

There was absolutely no support for the notion that staying home to watch hawks was important work. In our western society, such pointless sitting around qualified as pure laziness. Do-nothing people were bored, and boring. Couch potatoes watching TV.

Never mind that I didn't have a TV; I knew the stereotype. I could not entirely free myself of its stigma. At some deep level I thought that I ought to go back to work. But I could not figure out if that was what I truly wanted.

I had turned fifty this year. At least half my life was almost certainly over. What did I want to do with the rest of it?

I sighed again. I'd been sitting here awhile. Sunny's breathing had returned to normal and he shifted his front feet. Sunny was a patient horse, but even he was ready to move on. I patted his neck.

"You're right," I said aloud. "This isn't getting me anywhere."

It never did. No matter how many times I mulled it over, no answer emerged. In an effort to break the stalemate, I'd made a plan to ride along with Lucy Conners, who was currently practicing as a vet for our firm. This would be happening on Monday.

"Day after tomorrow, I'll have a better idea," I said finally.

Somehow I had the notion that I would be able to tell if being back in the saddle at work, so to speak, felt stimulating or claustrophobic, simply by accompanying Lucy on her rounds. In any case, it was the best idea I could come up with.

Laying the rein against Sunny's neck, I said, "Okay, let's go."

Sunny turned away from the view with alacrity. He knew my routines. Now we were headed home.

The horse marched purposefully, but without hurrying, across the flat little meadow and took the trail that headed downhill between the madrones. I glanced briefly at the dirt logging road which also led down the hill, but allowed Sunny's choice to stand. I would take the pretty trail home.

Chapter 2

THE PRETTY TRAIL WOUND down the hill gently, passing between broad-leafed trees, oaks, and redwoods, a swirling green kaleidoscope leading one to the heart of the forest. Mac and I had named it the "pretty trail" years ago, and the name had stuck. As I descended the branch trail from the Lookout headed for the junction to the pretty trail, I glanced automatically downhill at a hunter's blind in an oak tree. This blind had been here for many years—ever since I'd been riding these trails. I'd never seen anyone in it or near it. But I had the curious conviction that it was not deserted. My over-the-shoulder glance in its direction was, as always, uneasy. That blind made me uncomfortable.

Now we were in a redwood grove; the blind was hidden behind trees. I couldn't see much of anything. The woods were quiet; only the creak of my saddle and the crunch of Sunny's footfalls reached my ears. I stared at the trail in front of me, seeing the usual mix of horse hoofprints, deer tracks, pawprints, and human footprints. Everything quiet and peaceful. I could smell the rich dusty scent of the redwood duff, loamy and evocative of summer. A jay squawked high in the branch of a nearby oak tree. I turned my head to catch the flash of blue as he skipped across the air.

Crack! Loud and sharp, the distinct explosion of a gun, firing through the hills, not too far from us. Both Sunny and I flinched. I grabbed the saddle horn and got ready to stop Sunny if he bolted, but my little yellow horse didn't even spook. Apparently he'd heard gunshots before. I pulled him up and listened as the echo died away.

Nothing. No second shot. No voices. Nothing changed in the green world around me; nothing crashed, nothing moved. Deep in the forest as I was, I couldn't see far. The silence seemed absolute, as if the little critters of the woods were listening, too. I waited, listening. A squirrel chattered on the limb of a pine tree above me. I looked up. Then I squinted down the trail. Still nothing. Moments passed. Taking a deep breath, I bumped Sunny's sides with my heels, letting him step forward. My heart was pounding, but I didn't see what else to do. That shot had not come from very far away.

Sunny trooped down the hill, ears forward, shuffling his back feet a little, as he often did on descents. He didn't seem perturbed by the shot. On we went. My heart gradually slowed down. I'd heard shots in the woods before, many times. Usually at dawn or dusk, usually when I was home, sitting on my own front porch. I had never, that I could remember, heard a shot as I rode through the hills on a Saturday afternoon. Perhaps a poacher. It was the season for it. I thought of the hunter's blind. It was well behind me now, and I wasn't going back.

We were almost at the trail junction when Sunny's head came up and he halted suddenly. I looked where he was looking and saw motion through the trees, which quickly became a horse and rider loping towards us up the pretty trail.

The horse was a buckskin; the rider, I was quite surprised to see, was male. I rarely met men riding back here. Why, I wasn't sure. But virtually all of the equestrians I encountered were female, mostly riding solo.

In another second I'd recognized the guy. Jonah Wakefield, the resident trainer at Lazy Valley Stable. The fact that Jonah got to call himself a trainer had a lot to do with the fact that he was sleeping with the owner of Lazy Valley—Juli Barnes. Jonah had taken a six-week course with a well-known horse guru and now felt he was equal to anything when it came to breaking and training horses. Juli apparently liked him well enough to second this belief by calling him her trainer. The whole situation made a lot of us local horse folks roll our eyes.

If there'd been a way to avoid talking to Jonah, I would have been glad to take it. But the man had spotted me and pulled his horse up. Tipping his black cowboy hat—of course he would wear a black felt Stetson—he invited me to pass by.

I'd met Jonah before, but I could see by his face that he didn't recognize me. This was just fine with me. I smiled a small smile in his general direction, and clucked to Sunny. Obligingly Sunny stepped forward quietly, ready to pass the other horse. But the buckskin danced and skittered sideways towards us, determined to greet this newcomer. Jonah, who was wearing a long duster that went perfectly with the black hat—that is, if you like an affected wannabe cowboy style—allowed his horse to sidle up to Sunny and sniff his nose.

"He's just a baby," he said.

Right. I kept my opinion that he should make his baby mind to myself. Sunny ignored the buckskin, except to tip his ears backward. I bumped Sunny's face with my hand and his sides with my leg, and my steady little horse made to go on by.

"I wouldn't let him pin his ears like that," Jonah said.

Now this was a bit much. I had ignored his horse's genuinely bad manners and he felt free to criticize me for my horse's very mild response. Call me bad-tempered and hasty, but I couldn't quite keep my mouth shut.

"Is that right?" I said. "If I were you, I wouldn't allow my colt to nuzzle strange horses. If they don't happen to be as well broke as Sunny, your baby could get kicked." I smiled sweetly.

Jonah bared his teeth in a white flash that passed for a smile in return, but he didn't look pleased. "I'm a horse trainer," he said. Again he flashed the smile, no doubt sure that I would be both charmed and impressed. After all, he had a whole herd of middle-aged women who looked just like me and they all thought he was a big deal.

Unfortunately his quite handsome face cut no ice with me. I've never been all that impressed with handsome men, and I wasn't getting any more so in my old age.

"You're a trainer?" I said innocently. "I wouldn't have guessed it. Do you mind keeping your colt under control while I ride by. I don't need my good horse kicked." And, once more, I asked Sunny to step by the buckskin.

Sunny complied. Jonah didn't seem to know what to say to this. Although obviously nettled, he reined the prancing buckskin to the side. Just as I cleared him and made to head off down the pretty trail, he called after me. "Do you know Ross Hart?"

"Guy who trains at the Red Barn?" I said, pulling Sunny up once more.

"Yeah. I saw him down below, running his horse at warp speed. Looked like he was headed this way. You might want to keep an eye out."

"Right," I said. "Did you hear that shot?"

"What shot?" Jonah Wakefield sounded puzzled.

"I heard a shot. A minute or so ago. From down there somewhere." I waved my hand in a downhill direction.

"Nope. Didn't hear a thing." Jonah's horse was dancing with impatience and he gave up trying to control it. "See ya," and he flashed me a meant-to-be charming smile at the same moment that he let the buckskin whirl around and resume careering up the hill. I watched his retreating form and shrugged.

Sunny and I continued down the pretty trail, with me quite earnestly hoping I was done encountering people for the day. But I'd only rounded one corner when an angry buzz in the distance made me flinch. I knew that buzz; I knew what it meant. And it was rapidly approaching.

Somewhat desperately I searched the terrain around me, looking for a safe spot. I didn't have much time. That slope up ahead next to the curve would have to do. I kicked Sunny up to the trot, reached the wide spot, and reined him up the hill and off the trail. Sunny complied calmly; the approaching mechanical snarl didn't seem to bother him.

In another second it was visible, engine roaring as it blasted up the hill, a little motorcycle of the type called a dirt bike. I recognized the bearded rider as the guy I'd seen before. I was clearly visible on my bright yellow horse, standing by the side of the trail, but the biker neither paused nor slowed. He came on full speed and blew by me in a rush of noise and wind. I caught a glimpse of some sort of elation on his face as he sped by.

Resisting the strong urge I felt to flip the biker off, I patted Sunny's neck in gratitude for his completely calm, unflustered demeanor, and stepped him back down on the trail in the wake of the disappearing motorbike.

"This is it," I said out loud. "I am absolutely not going out riding on the weekends ever again. I never see anybody up here during the week."

The sound of my own voice was reassuring, as was the sight of Sunny's yellow ears, pricked forward as he paced steadily down the trail. I tried to refocus on the green world around me, but I could feel my jangled nerves jumping restlessly, alert for trouble. The shot and the dirt bike had definitely rattled me.

As I passed the turnoff to the "swingset trail," so named because it led past an abandoned swingset in the woods, I caught the flash of a horse and rider disappearing through the trees in the distance, headed away from me, going uphill, toward the top of the ridge. Too far away and behind too many trees to have any idea who it was; the horse looked like a sorrel. Whoever it was, was going at the high lope, and would soon top the ridge, either aiming for Moon Valley or Tucker Pond. I peered curiously at the dust hanging in the air, but the rider was gone.

On we trooped, steadily downhill. Redwoods and oaks made a leafy green wall of trees around me. Light slanted through, seeming to sparkle in brilliant flecks on the grass that fringed the trail. Soon we would reach the junction with the dirt logging road and the meadow full of pampas grass that I had looked down on from the ridge trail. This meadow was criss-crossed with the tracks of dirt bikes—I sincerely hoped that all would be quiet there today.

Looking over my left shoulder, I saw the forked shape of the landmark tree silhouetted against the sky. Sunny and I were behind it now. I imagined how it looked from my front porch, solitary on the ridgeline. We were deep in the wild woods now, the heart of the green world.

I glanced behind me. Nothing but trees and shafts of golden late afternoon light. But I had the sense that someone was watching me. I tried to shrug it off, reminding myself that I often had this feeling when I rode solo through the hills. Many times I had imagined the waiting, watchful eyes of a cougar fixed on us from some shadowy place. Once, long ago, I had met a mountain lion on these trails.

But it wasn't the wild critters who were worrying me now.

Sunny walked out, eager to get home. We passed the junction with the logging road and I looked idly up its two ruts. Surely those were fresh tire tracks. Not a motorcycle. A truck or a car. The road was rough; it must have been a four-wheel-drive vehicle. I wondered who had driven up there.

We were in the scrubby meadow full of clumps of rustling pampas grass. I remembered the day I had galloped across this meadow in the teeth of a blowing storm and reached down to stroke Sunny's neck. "You got me through that one, didn't you, boy?"

Sunny ignored me. His stride was rhythmic and relaxed as he plowed steadily through the loose sandy ground and up a hill. He knew where he was going. He didn't need my encouragement or my pats. Solid-minded little Sunny knew how to take care of himself.

I smiled and felt my shoulders drop a fraction. Maybe we were going to get through the rest of this ride undisturbed. So far it hadn't exactly been my most relaxing horseback jaunt.

The trail curved through a grove of madrones and oaks, headed toward the next ridge. I took in the brilliant blue of the sky behind the sharp-edged, shiny, green leaves and smelled the trail dust. Up ahead I could see the bright openness of another small meadow.

And suddenly Sunny came to a stop. His head came up; his ears pricked so sharply that they almost touched at the tips. And then he nickered.

Now this was surprising. Sunny didn't nicker under saddle. Not once that I could remember had he done this. I craned to see ahead through the trees. One day last spring Sunny and I had met a coyote pup at this very spot. Both horse and coyote had been intrigued with each other—but Sunny had certainly not nickered.

I couldn't see anything. I bumped with my heels, but Sunny stood as if rooted to the spot and nickered again. This time an answering nicker rang out. Up ahead, in the meadow.

Once again I bumped with my heels against Sunny's sides and clucked to him. Sunny's head lifted a fraction more, and he stepped forward. Both of us stared intently down the trail, peering through the screen of trees as we walked on. There was another horse there somewhere.

In another fifty feet we emerged from the shrubbery into the sunny wide-open golden grass of what I called the "warm meadow." Our trail ran right through the middle of this meadow until it reached the spot where four single-track paths came together. Standing near this junction, grazing, was a white horse, wearing a saddle and a bridle. She lifted her head and nickered softly when she saw us.

I stared. Sunny stared. Surely that was Dolly. I recognized the mare, and the saddle. But where was Jane? It didn't seem like her to turn her horse loose to graze dragging the bridle reins.

"Hey, Dolly," I said in a conversational tone. "Where's your person?"

The mare lifted her head and looked at me. I wasn't exactly expecting an answer to my question, and yet it seemed as if the horse had heard and understood.

She took a couple of steps down the trail, and then her hoof came down on the dragging reins, jerking her in the face. Dolly's head flew up, but she was an old horse and she'd been around. She lifted her hoof, releasing the rein, and kept on down the trail at a walk. I followed her.

Past the trail junction, on down the valley. Sunny eyed the trail that led to home, but followed the mare fairly willingly. I wondered if I should get off and catch the riderless horse, but Dolly seemed to be managing okay.

"Jane!" I called. The sound seemed to echo off the hills around me. No one answered.

This was weird. Where the hell was Jane?

And then Dolly stopped. Her head went down. I rode past the small scrubby pine tree by the side of the trail and saw the figure lying on the ground behind the tree. Blue jeans, boots, dark blond hair streaked with gray—face down. Dolly was sniffing her hair.

In a second I was off of Sunny and tethering him by the reins to a tree branch. Sunny stood quietly while I stepped past the white mare and reached down for Jane. I turned her over.

Jane's body was heavy in my arms, her head rolled back limply. Her eyes were open, not seeing me, glazed, the pupils fixed. I knew she was dead, even as my eyes searched frantically for a cause. Had she had a heart attack or a stroke, fallen and broken her neck?

But no, the bright red blood splotching the small hole in her chest gave the answer. My heart pounded; I could feel a strange rushing in my ears. Even as I pressed my fingers to Jane's neck to feel for a pulse, I sat down abruptly on the dry grass. Jane had been shot. And no doubt it was the shot I heard.

I was having a hard time looking at her sightless eyes. I closed my own and tried to focus on feeling for the heartbeat in her carotid artery. Nothing.

She was dead. What to do? My head was spinning.

You will not pass out, I told myself firmly. I looked around.

The familiar scrub was suddenly ominous. The person who had

fired this shot could be hiding anywhere. They could be watching me right now. I took a deep breath.

Panic would help nothing. Running away would serve no purpose.

Pay attention, I told myself. Listen.

I listened. Birds rustled in a nearby live oak. Dolly chomped a bite of grass. Sunny's ears were pricked forward, watching me. No immediate threat presented itself.

What to do?

I dug my cell phone out of my pocket, already knowing it wouldn't work. There was no reception in these little pockets in the hills. No signal.

That way, I glanced to the west, was a group of big houses, not too far away, a newish upscale subdivision. But I knew no one there, and what about my horse?

Jane was dead, no hurry would help her. I made a snap decision. My cell phone would work at the Lookout. If I loped, I could be there in less than ten minutes. Sunny and I would stay together. Somehow that felt right.

What about Dolly? The mare was grazing calmly, but who knew what would happen while I was gone. I got up and walked over to her, patted her neck, and picked up her reins. Tying them in a simple knot around a tree branch, I stepped back. Dolly regarded me calmly. It wasn't a great idea to tie horses by the bridle reins, but I didn't see what else to do.

I turned from the mare and approached my own little horse, who bumped me with his muzzle. Untying him, I flipped the reins over his head. Putting my left foot in the stirrup, I swung aboard, giving my usual inward thanks that he was only 14.3. "Come on, Sunny," I said out loud.

I sent him straight ahead down the trail, first at the walk, looking back over my shoulder to see that Dolly stayed calm. She did. I kicked Sunny up to a trot and then let him break into a lope. We were headed to the Lookout.

Chapter 3

SUNNY LOPED STEADILY DOWN the flat sandy trail that led across the warm meadow. The motion of his galloping stride was soothing, wiping some of the fear and shock from my mind. The landscape streaked by in a blur; the wind of our passing brushed my face, lifting my hair and Sunny's mane. The meadow narrowed into a small valley, fringed by oaks and willows. Sunny's hoof-beats drummed louder as the valley closed in ahead, meeting the north slope of a ridge. I could feel the chill as the air temperature dropped. We were in the "cold valley."

I checked Sunny to a scrambling trot as we forded the dry creek-bed, home of a tumbling stream in the winter, and then let him pick up the lope again as we started up the hill. We were in the deep shade of the redwoods now, lunging steadily upwards, and I could feel Sunny beginning to puff. The thrust of his hindquarters rocked me forward and I urged him with my body as his rhythmic gait devoured the slope.

We emerged from the redwoods into a tumble of leafy green berry vines, oak trees, and currant bushes, the trail leading steadily uphill throughout. I could see the three-way trail junction ahead on the ridgeline; late afternoon sunshine slanted through the trees, lancing into my eyes. I clucked to Sunny and bumped him with my heels and he loped on, his sides moving in and out with his huffing breath.

As we topped the ridge I pulled him up under the big oak tree in the flat where the three trails met. Maybe my cell phone would work. I dug it out of the side pocket of my cargo pants, but a quick glance showed me "no signal." The Lookout, then.

Motion out of the corner of my eye made my head jerk to the right. A hiker was coming down the sun-splashed ridge trail. A heavyset middle-aged man in walking shorts with a stout yellow Lab on a leash. The man carried a machete in his right hand and wore a small pack on his back.

The man saw me at the same moment I saw him, and halted. For a second our eyes met. I'm not sure what he saw in mine. Should I confide in this stranger? Ask for help? Send him down to guard the body? Warn him not to go down there? See if he had a cell phone that would work from here?

These thoughts raced through my mind in the few seconds that my no doubt frantic gaze rested on the guy. I took in the muscled legs under the stout body and the wagging tail on the big dog. The machete in the right hand gave me pause. I could read nothing in the man's expression—nothing at all.

I made a split-second decision. I didn't know this guy. For all I knew he was the killer. I would ride on to the Lookout and call for help.

Without a word I wheeled Sunny and trotted off down the trail that led to the Lookout.

Sunny moved forward reluctantly. I could feel his displeasure. We'd been up this trail once before this afternoon and Sunny had been in favor of going home then. Now, tired, out of breath, and sweaty, he was being asked to lope up the steep hill to the Lookout.

I clucked to him and thumped him with my heels and Sunny got the message. It was time to try. He put some real effort into lunging up the final ascents. I tried to keep my weight forward over his withers where it was easiest for him to carry and to stay with him as he scrambled uphill. I could feel his adrenaline pushing him as we charged forward and upward, the forest a blur around us.

When we broke into the clearing that topped the Lookout hill, I pulled the horse up. Digging my cell phone out of my pocket as Sunny gasped for air, his nostrils wide and red, I started to dial 911 and then stopped. How was I going to describe where this body was? I pictured the dubious voice of officialdom listening to my story. And without wasting another second I dialed a number I still remembered. Jeri Ward's cell phone.

Jeri Ward was an old friend, and also a detective with the Santa Cruz County Sheriff's Department. If anybody could help me, she could. I just hoped she hadn't changed her cell phone number. I hadn't talked to Jeri in almost ten years.

She answered on the first ring: "Jeri Ward here."

"Jeri, it's Gail. Gail McCarthy. I'm out riding in the woods and I found a woman shot. She's dead."

"Are you sure?"

"Yes, she's dead."

"And she's definitely been shot?"

"Yes."

"Where is she?"

"That's the hard part."

I was thinking fast. The logging road came out on a country crossroad not too far from my house. I described the spot to Jeri, who said she'd meet me there in ten minutes.

"I'm not sure if I can make it there in ten minutes," I told her. "I had to ride to the top of a hill to get a signal to call you. But I'll be there as soon as I can."

As soon as I ended the call, I turned Sunny and walked him back down the logging road. Sunny was still puffing hard—sweat dripped off his neck—but walking downhill would not hurt him. The logging road proceeded at a fairly gentle grade, staying high on the ridgeline and then winding gradually down the hill, passing big flats that were once log decks. The views of the local mountains were spectacular. From one spot I could see the ridge I lived on, and make out the triangular shape of my front porch gable. Usually this was a sight that I paused to take in. Not today.

Today I asked Sunny to walk briskly down the road, my thoughts on the shooting rather than the scenery. And yet, why would anyone shoot Jane? Jane, who was just out for a pleasant Saturday afternoon trail ride. Like me.

The thought caused me to look over my shoulder. Whoever had shot Jane might still be somewhere about. My mind went back to the gunshot I'd heard…and the various people I'd seen. Had one of those people fired that shot?

If so, I reflected, the gun would have to be a pistol. No one I saw had been packing a rifle or had any way to conceal one. I had no idea if the shot I'd heard had been a pistol or a rifle.

Who had I seen besides Jane? I counted them off in my mind. Sheryl Silverman, Jonah Wakefield, someone on a sorrel horse loping away, the bearded dirt bike rider, and a hiker with a dog and a machete. Could one of these be the killer?

I was so absorbed in my thoughts and the steady rhythm of bumping heels I was using to keep Sunny moving briskly that I almost didn't see the camper. Parked behind a tree well off the road at the edge of one of the log decks, the battered old vehicle looked to have a wonderful view of the surrounding hills. I checked Sunny for a moment and stared.

The ancient truck looked like a four-wheel drive. This must have been the author of the fresh tire tracks I'd seen. I looked down. Yep—tracks leading into this clearing. Did that camper have a perfect view of the meadow where I'd found Jane?

The thought gave me an instant shiver down my spine. I could see no one; the vehicle looked shut up tight. But I wanted away from here—badly. I kicked Sunny up to a trot.

Trotting downhill was not Sunny's forte. Thick-bodied and coarse, he moved like a small draft horse and wallowed from side to side as he lumbered down the hill, occasionally stumbling. I kept him trotting anyway. He'd caught his breath and I knew from experience he wouldn't fall down. Sunny might be a touch clumsy in some ways but he'd covered a lot of country in his life. He knew how to take care of himself.

Down we went, the road zigging and zagging back and forth along the ridge. We came to the pampas grass meadow and Sunny tried to take the trail that led to the warm meadow and on to home. I reined him firmly down the road and urged him to trot faster. By my reckoning it had been more than ten minutes already.

Down and down—we were in the shadows now; the westering sun was nearing the ridge. I could see the busy road ahead, and there where the logging road met the street were two dark green sheriff's sedans. Jeri Ward was here.

The road leveled out and I urged Sunny to the lope.

I could see the small knot of people standing by the two cars— Jeri's blond head was evident. All faces swung in my direction and various surprised eyes took in the sight of my approach on a galloping yellow horse, mane and tail flying. Jeri smiled as I pulled up.

"Hey Gail—quite an entrance."

"Hi Jeri." I was almost as out of breath as my horse. "Are you all coming with me?" I glanced at the two other uniformed male deputies.

"Just me, for now." Jeri looked over her shoulder at the men. "Wait here. I'll be right back." And then, to me, "Will he take double?"

I'd been thinking about this. "Yes. But we'll have to walk him."

"Of course."

Jeri approached Sunny's left side. I kicked my foot out of the left stirrup and she reached up and put her left foot in. Grabbing the back of the cantle with her right hand and the saddle horn with her left, she swung her right leg over Sunny's butt and hauled herself upward. I leaned forward to give her room. In a moment

I could feel her straighten up behind me. Sunny grunted but held his ground. The two male deputies stared.

"Okay," Jeri said. "Let's go."

I turned Sunny up a trail that led west, over a nearby hill—a shortcut to the warm meadow. In a minute we were in the trees and out of sight of the deputies. Sunny trudged along, bearing our double weight stoically, as was his way. Jeri's shoulders bumped mine occasionally; I glanced down to see her neatly manicured hands gripping the cantle behind me

"Can you just leave those guys like that?" I asked her.

I could feel her smile. "Yep. I'm their boss."

"You are?"

"We haven't seen each other in awhile. I'm Detective Sergeant in Charge of Homicide for Santa Cruz County now."

"Oh," I said. "You got promoted." When last I'd seen Jeri, she'd been one of several detectives in the Santa Cruz County Sheriff's Department.

"That's right."

"You can still ride, anyway," I said. "Do you still have ET?"

ET had been Jeri's horse when I knew her. A sweet, gentle older gelding, he had one blind eye, and looked something like a giraffe crossed on a dachshund—not at all fancy but a good reliable trail horse. It was only because I knew that Jeri had a horse and could ride that I'd assumed we could ride Sunny double to the site of the murder.

"No," Jeri said, "ET died when he was thirty. But I've got another sweet old horse now. A gray gelding, used to be a team roping horse. Called Gray Dog. So, Gail, what's the deal here? Where are we going? Where's the victim?"

"You'll see," I said. "We're close now."

Sunny topped the rise and I could see the warm meadow shining golden in front of us in the last late afternoon sunshine. It looked entirely peaceful and serene, and the thought of Jane's body, killed by a shot, lying in that shimmering bleached grass was deeply disconcerting. I took a breath, about to speak, and was interrupted by a shrill whinny. Dolly had spotted us. Sunny whickered back.

"That's the victim's horse," I said to Jeri. "I tied the mare to a tree. Looks like she's still there."

"Do you know this victim?" Jeri's voice behind my ear was clipped and stern, her cop voice.

"Yes. She's Jane Kelly. I met her earlier this afternoon on her horse and we chatted for a while. Everything seemed entirely normal. After I left her, maybe twenty minutes later, I heard a shot. I'm pretty sure it was the shot that killed her."

Sunny trudged through the dry grass of the meadow, following the sandy trail. I could see the scrubby pine ahead that screened the body. A flash of white behind the tree was Dolly's white coat. I took another deep breath.

And then we were past the tree and could see the form lying on the ground. Jane's body lay as I'd left it, face up, sightless eyes staring at the sky. The red splotch on her chest was immediately evident. I pulled Sunny up.

Both Jeri and I were quiet for a moment. I could feel Jeri's eyes taking in the scene.

"Is this how you found her?" she said at last.

"Almost. Her horse was loose and I ran into it back there a ways." I motioned back in the direction we'd come from. "The mare actually led us to Jane. I pulled Sunny up about where we're standing now, and then tied him to that tree over there." I pointed. "Jane was lying just where she is, except face down. I turned her over—I couldn't tell what was wrong with her. When I saw the bullet hole, I knew. I checked for a pulse and there was none. Her eyes were glazing, pupils were fixed." I swallowed. "I knew she was dead. My cell phone wouldn't work from here, so I tied the mare to a tree and rode to the top of a hill to call you. Then I rode back a different way to meet you. That's about it."

Jeri took this in. I could feel her shift her weight and I took my left foot out of the stirrup and leaned forward so that she could climb down. I watched her walk forward and peer closely at Jane's body, though she didn't touch anything. "I need to get the crime scene guys here pronto," she muttered. "Gail, where are we exactly? What's the closest street?" Jeri looked around.

All that met the eye was brush, dry grass, and mixed oak and pine trees, but appearances were deceiving.

"There's a subdivision right behind those trees." I pointed to the west. "The closest house is only a hundred yards away."

"Why didn't you go there to phone?" Jeri asked, looking up at me.

I shrugged. "I don't know any of those people. They're all big fancy houses. What was I going to do with my horse?" What I thought, but didn't say, was that the residents of that subdivision were very anti-equines and had been known to call the sheriff's department on any hapless trail riders they spotted on their pristine street. I had no desire to make their acquaintance, emergency or not. "Jane was dead," I added. "No amount of hurry was going to help her."

Jeri nodded, almost imperceptibly. "How do I get to this subdivision?"

"The easiest way is to backtrack to that trail junction in the meadow. If you take the trail that leads that way," I motioned again to the west, "you'll come out on the street that runs through there. It's called Storybook Way."

Jeri dug her radiophone out of her pocket and appeared ready to call the troops. Quickly I said, "Jeri, I need a favor."

She looked up.

"I need to go home. It's getting late and Blue and Mac will be worried. I need to put this poor horse away." I gestured at the dried sweat on Sunny's shoulders. "Can you let me go home now and stop around later and take my statement?"

Jeri's eyes met mine and I knew she was remembering the other times we'd worked together. Her chin moved up and down slightly, that same almost imperceptible nod. "Sure," she said. "You go ahead. I'll get the crime scene guys here, and get them started, then I'll come by your place."

"Thanks," I said.

"One thing," she added. "Where does this horse live?" And she pointed at Dolly.

"Lazy Valley Stable," I said.

"Really." Jeri half smiled. "That's right next door to the pasture where I keep Gray Dog. I'll make sure she gets home. I'll see you in a couple of hours."

"Thanks," I said again. And wheeled Sunny before she could change her mind. I did not look back, even when Dolly nickered wistfully after me. I wanted out of there. The sight of Jane's still form and sightless eyes was troubling me in ways I hardly understood. Only an hour ago Jane had been alive and full of fight. It seemed almost impossible that she had been snuffed out so quickly and finally.

Sunny moved briskly down the trail, almost breaking into a trot. He didn't hesitate when Dolly called after him. Sunny, like me, wanted to go home, and he knew the way.

We marched across the warm meadow, Sunny's buttermilk-colored ears pricked sharply forward. His pace increased as I allowed him to take the trail that led north, over the next ridge, and on to home. I watched his head bob rhythmically up and down as he trudged steadily up the grade, eagerness in every inch of his demeanor. We topped the ridge and were instantly on a narrow winding sidehill trail in the shadows of a mixed forest.

Along the ridge the path wound and twisted, skirting narrow washes and dodging massive tree trunks. The last sunlight dappled patches of berry vines, wild roses, and poison oak. I ducked the long twining arms that reached for me, ducking particularly carefully for the very large, solid overhanging branch that Mac and I called "the head-bonker tree."

Sunny's eager walk verges into a jog from time to time, but I check him and he complies. Let alone that jigging isn't good manners and annoys me, this narrow sidehill trail traverses a steep slope and a foot put wrong could be dangerous. Thus we walk briskly, but we walk.

The tangled woods go gliding by; I ride, half in a daze, my mind on Jane's murder. Who could have done this? And why?

I realize that I can't possibly have any idea why, as little as I know about Jane. But surely Jane had just told me that she'd stolen Doug back from Sheryl Silverman, and I had met Sheryl on the trail, headed in Jane's direction, very shortly before I'd heard the shot. Sheryl had saddlebags tied behind her saddle. I remembered the fringe. It was entirely possible that a pistol had been in the saddlebags.

Resolving to tell Jeri this when I saw her, I checked Sunny at the top of a very steep downhill slither, forcing him to take his time. Sunny tucked his butt under him and half walked, half slid down the steep drop, completely calm and composed. We rode this trail often and Sunny knew all its minor obstacles and took them in stride. Sunny took most things in stride. It was his nature.

He paced through the eucalyptus grove at the bottom of the descent, stepping over downed trunks and branches, following the shadow of the path. I glanced to my left. There, visible in glimpses through the peeling, pinkish trunks were the gigantic pseudo-mansions of the subdivision on Storybook Road. This narrow trail I followed had been created by some enterprising equestrians when the pricey subdivision had gone in several years ago. Previous to that event, we had all ridden across a big meadow on a lovely winding dirt road to get to the ridge trails and the Lookout. But rich people and their houses had come and the people were emphatically anti-horse. I could still remember the irate shouting voice of one wealthy suburbanite threatening me with imminent arrest were I to dare to take my horse up his road ever again.

I hadn't dared. This sort of conflict took all the fun out of riding the trails, for me. But a year later I had stumbled on the sidehill trail, when Mac and I were out hiking. And from then on, I used it often as a route to the ridge.

As far as I knew, very few other equestrians knew about this little trail. I didn't know who had created it. I didn't advertise it; I'd quite carefully not mentioned it to Jane. It had occurred to me that the land the trail crossed might well be owned by the suburbanites and if they knew we traversed it, they might object. But the trail was hidden from their sight, and I had an idea that few of them ever left their giant houses, complete with terraces and manicured lawns, to venture into the wild woods. Thus I kept quiet about the sidehill trail, and quiet while I was on it, and hoped to be left to use it in peace.

It struck me now that I would avoid mentioning my sidehill trail to Jeri. No point in having a bunch of sheriff's deputies tromping through, and I doubted it could relate to Jane's murder. But I would tell Jeri about the poacher's blind, I thought. I had such a funny feeling about that spot. We would have to check and see if there was a line of sight from the blind to the meadow where Jane had been shot.

We... I shook my head. I wasn't investigating this, Jeri was. But the "we" stayed in my mind.

I had probably been the last person to speak to Jane. That thought struck me like a bullet, as Sunny tossed his head and started down another dropoff. I bumped the horse with my hand, gently and automatically, and he gathered himself to shuffle down the steep slope. But my thoughts were on Jane, on our conversation, what there had been of it. I was trying to remember every detail, knowing I'd need to repeat it to Jeri. There had been the story of Jane and Doug and Sheryl, and something about Tammi Martinez and Ross Hart. And all those complaints about trail access. Jane had definitely talked about the bearded dirt bike rider, I remembered with a half start. And I'd seen him today.

Sunny was descending the bottom of the slope, winding between oaks and pines. Ahead of me was the bright gold of another small meadow. I could hear the whiz of cars rushing up and down the busy road on the other side of the tangled fringe of trees and brush. Hidden from the public eye by the kind vegetation, we paced across the meadow and through a small grove of oaks to stand on the shoulder of the road, waiting to cross.

Waiting and waiting, actually. It took what seemed like hours, but was probably only five minutes, for the road to be clear in both directions. I kicked Sunny up to a trot and we crossed quickly, before a car could bear down on us. The road was truly dangerous, and I always took it seriously. It had claimed lives before now, and was capable of doing so again. I didn't forget.

Once across, I headed past a big Monterey pine and up the slope between twisted live oaks. Straight ahead was my front gate. Pointing Sunny up the hill, I told him, "Let's go home."

Chapter 4

I RODE THROUGH MY FRONT gate and glanced automatically up the drive to see that Blue's pickup was gone. Wondering in a vague way where everybody was, I let Sunny march briskly up the hill to the barn. Henry and Plumber nickered from their respective corrals. Henry, I was pleased to see, looked quite normal. Three months out from colic surgery and I still could not suppress my reflexive, anxious glance at my son's red horse. Henry's doing fine, I told myself. Don't worry about him. You've got other things to worry about.

Climbing off Sunny, I unsaddled him, brushed him, and hand grazed him a little on the patch of rough lawn that I watered to keep it green in the dry season. Sunny munched happily, but I only gave him a minute.

"Sorry, son," I said, tugging his head up and leading him back to his corral. "I need to move along."

I distributed a flake of mixed alfalfa/grass hay to each horse, and then trudged up the hill toward the house. Or houses, rather. I still couldn't quite get used to it. There, in a flat spot next to the vegetable garden, where Blue had once parked his travel trailer when he first moved out here, sat a small cottage. Shingled all over with cedar shake and roofed in green tin, the same as the main house, the new house looked like a little sister. Resisting the urge to sink down in the comfortable rocking chair just inside the big windows, I pushed my weary legs up the hill to my original dwelling.

Opening the door, I called out, "Anybody home?"

No answer except a small meow. I glanced down to see Shadow, our little black female cat, twining herself around my ankles.

"Just you, huh?" I said, reaching to pet her.

Walking over to the table, I saw the note. "Gone shopping. Be back soon. Mac (and Blue)." Written in my son's angular printing. I smiled. All was well with my family.

A sigh of relief escaped me, though I hadn't consciously been aware I was worried. But Jane... I shook my head. I could not rid myself of the memory of Jane's sightless eyes.

Stepping over to the stove, I lit the burner and filled the stainless steel kettle with water. Tea. That's what I needed. A cup of tea.

As I placed the kettle on the stove, I leaned back for a second, taking in the room around me, trying to absorb the peace of home.

Familiar and friendly, the rough-sawn knotty pine that lined the walls and open-beam ceiling glowed apricot gold in the evening light that filtered in through the large, south-facing windows and lit up the worn Oriental rug on the red-brown mahogany floor. Though the rug was old, it was new to this room. Blue and I had inherited it when his father had died. Blue's mother, who had died a year previously, had loved and collected various exotic treasures and this rug was one of hers. Our old rug being worn to tatters, we had installed the "new" one recently. Its formal but faded rust red and lapis blue patterns looked just right on the scuffed floor.

My eyes moved from the rug to the black woodstove on the gray river-rock hearth; the stove was silent and cold now, but gave the promise of a glowing fire in the winter days ahead. A Navajo-patterned blanket covered the couch next to the stove and a moss-green claw-footed armchair rested under a pair of Japanese woodblock prints on the wall. A round table in the corner by the kitchen and a desk with a computer on the far side of the room completed the accoutrements necessary for life.

The kettle hissed its readiness and I turned and made my tea, adding a little milk and sugar. Carrying the steaming blue willow cup, I made my way out on the porch and sat down, my eyes on the skyline.

Sitting in the chair, looking out at the opposite ridge, my horizon, my gaze rests on the landmark tree, lit up like a golden antler against the shadowed green of the ridgeline behind it. For a moment all my whirling thoughts subside and I remember riding along the ridge this afternoon, gazing at the landmark tree from the far side, seeing it outlined against the sky, knowing my porch lay beyond that, on a distant ridgeline.

In that second, peace wraps itself around me. For a brief moment I forget about the horror of Jane's body and the frantic maelstrom of events which is bound to follow soon. I stare at the familiar sight of the landmark tree on the ridge, sip my steaming tea, and let my thoughts wander in their usual paths.

I sit here often in the evening, fascinated by the notion that once, not so long ago, I stood on the opposite ridgeline, adrift in the wild, green world, looking back at my home on this ridge. Why this fascinates me I don't know.

Staring at the well-known landscape of the ridge, I pick out the tossing heads of the eucalyptus forest, the route of the ridge trail, the lofty pines behind the landmark tree, the silhouetted redwood grove that marks the site of the Lookout. I know virtually every inch of this scenery that I see from my porch. I have ridden and hiked the trails that trace the opposite ridge for many years, in all seasons. My fascination with it has never ended.

And now...I take another sip of tea while my mind swings inevitably back to Jane's body, lying by the side of the trail in the warm meadow. My eyes search out the particular oak tree crowns that I know rise over that meadow. Jeri and her crew are there now, investigating the scene of the crime. Soon Jeri will be here, ready to take my statement. Soon Blue and Mac will be home and I will need to tell them what has happened.

I take another sip of tea and feel a tide of protest rising inside of me. I don't want this. I want to contemplate the ridge in peace. I do not want this dark shadow of murder hanging over the peaceful landscape that I love. I want Jane alive and well and riding back to Lazy Valley Stable in the evening light. This blight, this evil, seems to pollute the beauty of the view, and my life, in an almost visible way. I can feel it in my bones, fear and anger mixing, in a way that makes my jaw clench.

For a second I stare hard at the ridgeline, aware of the sound of Blue's pickup truck coming up the driveway. Then I set my teacup down and stand up, a sense of resolution growing. I'm not sure where it will lead, but I know one thing. I'm not standing still for this evil. I'm fighting.

Chapter 5

THE SIGHT OF THE DARK green pickup parking in its place indicated Blue and Mac's imminent return. I had barely rinsed my teacup and turned toward the back door when they came barreling into the house, Freckles at their heels, all loud, friendly voices and wagging tails. I greeted my son and husband and patted the dog and wondered how to begin.

"What's wrong, Mama?" Mac, always intuitive, had spotted my strained expression.

"How was your ride?" asked Blue.

"Not good," I said.

"Is Sunny all right?" Mac asked quickly. Henry's colic and resulting surgery had made a deep impression. Mac's eyes went instantly to the cantaloupe-sized, round gray stone on the mantel, the enterolith that had been removed from Henry's large intestine. The ten thousand dollar rock, Blue and I called it.

"Sunny's fine," I said reassuringly. "But I found a woman by the trail." I swallowed. There was just no good way to put this. "She'd been shot. She was dead."

"Oh no." Blue's face got very still.

Mac's eyes were wide, with excitement as much as shock, I judged. At eleven years of age the tragedies of unknown others were not personal to him.

"Who shot her?" he asked. "Did you know her?"

"I knew her slightly. Her name was Jane Kelly." I didn't mention I'd been chatting with her less than an hour before she died. "She had a horse. No one knows who shot her. But since I found her, I called the sheriffs. And Jeri Ward is going to be here soon to take my statement."

"What's that?" Mac asked.

"I just need to tell Jeri everything that happened. She'll record it," I answered. I could see headlights coming up the driveway as I spoke. Daylight was ebbing fast. "There she is now."

"Why don't you take her over to the other house," Blue suggested. "Mac and I will make spaghetti for dinner."

"I'll make the meatballs," Mac said instantly. He liked cooking—especially things he enjoyed eating.

"Fine," I said, relieved that Mac hadn't demanded to join Jeri and me. Slipping out the door before he could think of doing this, I met Jeri on the driveway. "Come on over to my new little shack," I greeted her. "We can be private there."

As I led Jeri across the porch of the new house and through the glass door and flipped on the lights, I was conscious of a sense of pride all out of proportion to the situation. Our new cabin was tiny, about five hundred square feet, and featured one small but airy main room, surrounded by windows, a half kitchen, a bathroom, and a bedroom for Mac. We had built it in anticipation of the time, soon to come, when sleeping on a futon on the floor of our bedroom would not be enough private space for our son, and already he spent much of his time in his new bedroom, though he wasn't quite ready to sleep there yet.

The click of the light switch lit a rough glass sconce shaped like a half moon above the door, and a hidden light in the alcove across the room. Jeri's mouth parted slightly as she gazed about. I grinned.

"This is great," she said. "Did you build it yourselves?"

"Mostly. Blue had a contractor friend who helped."

The room we stood in was twenty by twenty with a high open-beam ceiling lined with willow twigs. Windowed like a screen porch, with a floor of rough-planked hand-scraped hickory boards and walls plastered with orangey-gold clay, the room was both small and simple and yet oddly spacious and stark. In one corner was a raised alcove, defined by the deep red trunk of a madrone, which provided the corner pillar. A hanging scroll in the alcove showed grass blowing in the wind. There was little furniture—a wicker rocking chair and a simple futon couch which folded out to make a bed. A small burgundy-toned prayer rug lay in front of the couch and a cedar chest in the corner supported Blue's bagpipes.

"We call this the music room," I said. "It's where Blue plays his bagpipes. They're loud. It's a good thing we've got a separate house. Would you like a tour of the whole place before we start? It won't take long."

"Sure," Jeri said, still gazing about in apparent fascination.

I led the way to Mac's room, through the beaded curtain, and watched Jeri peer at the antique desk in front of the turquoise-blue wall, a special request of Mac's and his favorite color. Mac's bed had a rust-colored quilt and a wool blanket with a Native American design of galloping horses.

"The bathroom is the best part," I said. "Blue wanted a big shower."

The small bathroom boasted a handmade concrete counter with a beaten copper sink and a five-by-five walk-in shower, tiled in stone, with a glass-block exterior wall that filled the space with light.

"I love glass block," said Jeri, gazing at the wall somewhat wistfully. "This is great," she added.

"We had fun with it," I said, and led the way back to the main room.

Settling into the rocker, I watched Jeri take the end of the couch and bring out her small recorder. Her smooth blond head, sporting a neat, short cut and showing no gray, I noticed, was bent over for a minute as she fiddled with the dials. I felt a sudden rush of fondness, remembering all of our previous interactions. I liked Jeri Ward. We'd known each other in an off-again on-again way for twenty years. Somehow we had never become intimate friends, perhaps because neither she nor I was the type to make many close friendships. Nonetheless, I liked her very much, and sensed that the feeling was mutual.

"Did you find anything interesting in the woods?" I asked her.

"Not really. Not yet," she muttered, not looking up. "The scene-of-crime guys are still there." And then, "I just got back from Lazy Valley Stable. I had a guy from there come pick up the horse."

"Was it the trainer, Jonah Wakefield?"

"Yeah, that's what he said his name was. Young, dark, clearly thinks he's God's gift to women."

"That would be Jonah," I agreed. "Does he know Jane's dead?"

"It was pretty much impossible not to tell him," Jeri said. "Given that I had to put someone in charge of the horse. He doesn't know the woman's been shot or where she was found, though. I led the horse down to that spot where you met us and had him pick her up there."

"I saw Jonah riding in the woods this afternoon," I said. "Not five minutes after I heard the shot."

"Oh really." Jeri clicked a button. "Okay, this thing's on now. Go ahead and tell me what you saw."

I took a deep breath. "I was riding up the ridge trail this afternoon when I met Jane Kelly, riding her mare, Dolly. Probably about three o'clock, though I can't be sure."

"You knew her, right?"

"Yeah, I knew her. She was one of my veterinary clients when I was a practicing vet and I would sometimes see her when I was out riding. We stopped and talked awhile."

"Where were you, exactly?"

"That's hard to describe, unless you know the trails. I could draw you a map, maybe."

"That's a good idea," Jeri said. "But for now, let's just get your story."

I recounted Jane's and my conversation as faithfully as I could remember it. "She was upset about problems with trail access," I said, and I described the guy who sicced his dog on riders, the dirt bike rider, and the unknown folks who kept trying to block the trails. "She was pretty angry about all that. She said that she'd just moved her horse to Lazy Valley Stable because of the trail access issues—also she couldn't get along with the new manager of the Red Barn, or the resident trainer there."

"And that is?"

"Tammi Martinez is the manager and the trainer is a young guy named Ross Hart."

"Do you know these people?"

"Sort of. I know people who board at that barn and they talked about them. I've met them both out riding. Neither of them has been there long. Less than a year. The old owner is a real nice gal, but she moved away and hired this much younger woman to run the place. Tammi's tough." I decided to leave it at that.

"What about the trainer?"

"Ross Hart. There's talk about him, I guess; but there always seems to be talk about trainers. Ross rented a house just behind the boarding stable about six months ago, and started training and giving lessons at the barn. Rumor has it, he's sleeping with Tammi. Jane said that he'd been up to some stuff that he shouldn't—whatever that means. She also said that some of his former clients were now taking lessons from her and that she knew quite a bit more about training than Ross."

"Nice," Jeri commented.

I shook my head. "Jane was not exactly nice," I said. "She was very direct; a lot of people didn't like her. She and I always got along well, though I knew her very slightly."

"So, go on with the story," Jeri prompted. "Try to tell it in order, as it happened."

"Okay," I said. "Jane and I talked for a while, maybe ten minutes. She told me she had just moved her mare to Lazy Valley Stable, partly because they had better trail access and partly because of her issues with Tammi and Ross. I asked why she had moved her horse to the Red Barn to begin with, and she said because Sheryl Silverman, who boards at Lazy Valley, had stolen Jane's boyfriend, Doug Martin." I rolled my eyes. "I know Sheryl a little—stealing boyfriends and husbands is sort of business as usual for her. Anyway, Jane said that at this point she and Doug were back together and she didn't mind seeing Sheryl. She sort of smirked about it; I got the impression she felt kind of smug."

I thought a minute. "I can't recall that we talked of much else. Her horse was getting restless; we both rode on."

"Which way did she go?" Jeri asked.

"She rode down the ridge. From there she could take a turn that leads back to Lazy Valley, or she could ride down to the Red Barn. Judging by where I found her, though, she must have doubled back up the ridge," I added doubtfully.

"What did you do next?"

"I rode on towards the Lookout, where I was headed. I didn't see anyone until I ran into Sheryl Silverman, who was also riding down the ridge trail in the same direction Jane was going."

"Did you talk to Sheryl?"

"Briefly. I kind of teased her; I guess it was evil of me. I mentioned seeing Jane and Sheryl looked furious. Then we went our ways. I didn't think anything of it." I wondered whether to mention that Sheryl had been packing saddlebags that would have accommodated a pistol and decided not. Not yet, anyway.

"What then?"

"I rode to the Lookout, spent some time staring over Monterey Bay. Have you been there?"

"Yep." Jeri grinned. "It's amazing."

"One of my favorite places, " I agreed. "I ride there a lot."

"Did you see anyone?"

"Not while I was there. But when I rode back down the trail, headed for home, I heard a shot. I'm pretty sure it had to be the shot that killed Jane."

"Could you tell where it came from?"

"Not really. I was in a deep, wooded spot; I couldn't see much. The sound seemed to come from all around me, if you know what I mean. I had the sense it wasn't far away. It spooked me a little, but I do hear gunshots in the woods from time to time, especially in the fall. I assume it's poachers, hunting deer. I did wonder if the shot came from the old hunter's blind that's in an oak tree just off the trail to the Lookout."

Jeri nodded. "Then what?"

"I rode on. And in less than five minutes I ran into Jonah Wakefield, the trainer from Lazy Valley, riding a buckskin colt."

"Did you talk to him?"

"Very briefly. I asked him if he heard the shot and he said no, which I find hard to believe. He said that he'd seen Ross Hart riding fast, or something to that effect."

"Did you see Ross Hart?"

"No. I did see someone galloping up the hill that leads to the swingset trail, but I couldn't see who it was. A sorrel horse, that's all I know. That was after I ran into the bearded guy on the dirt bike, or after he almost ran into me."

I described this encounter to Jeri and said that the dirt bike rider had not paused.

"Then I rode on until I got to the meadow where I found Jane. First I saw her horse and then I found her. I rolled her over, like I told you, and saw she was dead." I swallowed, the memory of Jane's blank eyes still difficult for me to face. "My cell phone wouldn't work there," I went on firmly, "so I rode to the Lookout and called you. On the way I saw a middle-aged man walking a yellow Lab with a machete in one hand. I didn't speak to him or him to me."

I took a breath. "I rode down the logging road to meet you. On the way I saw an old camper parked out of sight at the edge of a log deck. I didn't see any people about. After that I met you down by the road." I took another breath and folded my hands in my lap. "I think that about covers it."

Jeri was silent a moment: I had the sense she was trying to assimilate everything I had just said. Just as she opened her mouth to speak, her cell phone rang.

"Jeri Ward here," she answered crisply.

She listened to the staccato rattle of a voice and said, "Where?" She listened some more and then said, "I'll be right there."

Even as she turned to me, she shoved the cell phone and recorder into her pockets. "Got to go," she said. "My guys have picked up a young guy with a twenty-two rifle, hiking down the logging road. Young guy didn't want to say what he was doing there, nor did he have any registration for the gun, so they took him in for questioning. I've got to go down to the office. I'll be in touch."

And before I could say much of anything else, Jeri Ward had let herself out the door and was gone.

Chapter 6

I WATCHED JERI'S HEADLIGHTS retreat down my driveway and sighed. Now I had to go face Blue and Mac. I really, really did not want to go over this story again. What I wanted was to sit down and have a quiet, peaceful drink and try to relax. Flicking off the lights in the little house, I walked across the porch, finding my way by the glow of the lamps in the house across the yard. As I stepped towards the lit-up windows, a plaintive meow by my feet made me jump.

"Tigger!" I said, a bit sharply, as the fluffy shape dodged between my legs. "Watch out."

Tigger meowed again, unrepentantly, and followed me to the house, where he once again slipped between my feet as I walked in the door. I watched his furry tiger-striped form waddle down the hall (Tigger was not a slender cat) and had to grin.

A small dark shadow leaped upon Tigger from the darkness of the bedroom doorway and suddenly both cats were wrestling on the floor. I stepped over them, reflecting that little black Shadow had been aptly named, and walked into the main room, where Blue and Mac had spaghetti sauce and meatballs simmering on the stove. Blue took one look at my face and turned to the counter to pour lemonade-colored liquid into a tumbler filled with ice.

"Would you like a drink?" he said.

"Thank you, thank you." I smiled at him. "And it's a margarita, my favorite. How did you know?"

"I just guessed." Blue grinned back at me.

I sank into the moss-colored armchair with a sigh. Mac was sitting on the couch, playing his electric-keyboard piano. Blue leaned on the counter and took a swallow of his drink, his eyes on me. "How did it go?" he asked.

"Okay," I said. "Would it be all right if I just sipped this drink for a while? I'm exhausted. I really don't want to go over it again right away."

"No problem." Blue smiled again and his eyes went to Mac. "It can wait."

I knew we were both thinking that firsthand descriptions of a murder victim were not what our sensitive eleven-year-old son needed to hear. At the moment Mac was so absorbed in his music that I sincerely doubted he knew I was in the room.

I sipped my drink and watched Mac play. Watched Blue watch us both. Slowly my mind detached. I felt as if I were removed, a disembodied presence observing a scene: boy making music.

Mac's long slender fingers move over the keyboard; his expression is intent. His left hand extemporizes chords while his right hand picks out a melody. He creates phrases and repeats them, invents variations and returns to his ground. The music he is playing is sonorous and pleasing and though I know he is making it up as he goes along, it sounds as if it is a piece he has practiced and played many times.

I watch Mac's face and his fingers; he occasionally meets my eyes and seems pleased to find that I am listening; mostly he is caught up in what he is doing. He looks focused and happy. I know from experience that he can and will play the piano for long periods of time, whether anyone is listening or not. Mac is an entirely self-taught musician.

Sipping my drink, I note Mac's curiously adult expression and his broadening shoulders. He has begun that steady progression that leads to young manhood, and I feel a stab of nostalgia for the days when he was truly a child. But this passes quickly in a burst of pure pride.

Once again I focus on my son's music, as he sits playing the piano. Lamplight falls around him, laying a pool of warmth on the faded Oriental rug at his feet, kindling a yellow-gold glow on the rough-sawn knotty plank walls behind him. Mac's hair is a cap of ruffled fawn-colored waves; his big long-lashed eyes still hold the magical innocence of a fairy changeling. He has not yet acquired the rigid patina of approaching adolescence.

Mac is making music, his own music, and I am here. I take another swallow of margarita and smile at Blue as I feel the tension melt slowly out of my body. Blue smiles back and I know we are thinking the same thing.

Mac is growing up and we are all here together. What more is there to ask? Tragedy may stalk the hills, as it prowls the world at large, but for the moment we are here together and safe.

— . —

IT WAS LATER, much later, that I awoke from a deep sleep with my heart pounding. I could not remember the dream, only that it had had something to do with a body, sightless eyes staring upward. I shuddered, rolled over, tried to go back to sleep, realized I needed to go to the bathroom.

Climbing out of bed, I tottered down the hall as I so often did in the middle of the night these days. Glancing at the clock, I saw it was two-thirty. Par for the course. I looked idly out the window and froze.

There it was again. That light. My hall windows looked out at the ridge; the same ridge I had traversed so many times on Sunny. I knew every inch of that view. I had stared at it from my house and covered it on my horse many, many times. Until a month ago, I had never seen this light.

As far as I knew there was no dwelling where the light glowed, flickering. If I moved a few steps to the left or right it vanished.

But from this one spot, for the last month, the light sparkled every night, hanging on the ridge in a place that I thought was populated only by trees and brush.

It wasn't a fire, the color was wrong for that, and though it flickered, it was too consistent. What in the world was a light doing out in the brush? Whose light was it? What was the point of it?

I stared and stared, my nose pressed to the glass, trying to determine exactly where it was in relation to landmarks that I recognized. Halfway up the ridge trail, it looked like…but there simply wasn't anything there. I had ridden up the ridge trail many times.

That thought brought another thought to mind. Could the mysterious light have anything to do with the murder? It was quite a ways from the spot where I had found Jane's body, of that I was sure, but maybe not so far from the place where I had chatted with her on the trail. It was hard to see what the connection might be, but one thing I knew. I had never seen this light before a month ago. Whatever it was, it represented a change.

An owl hooted softly, far away in the darkness. I could smell the damp loamy scent of autumn, breathing in through the open window. The strange light shone silently on the ridge. I shifted from foot to foot.

I gave the light one last look and headed for the bathroom. Tomorrow, I told myself, I'll work on it tomorrow.

Chapter 7

AT SEVEN O'CLOCK THE NEXT morning the light was still there. It sparkled in the trees, dimmed by dawn's gray light, but still visible. It struck me that I had never looked for the mystery light by day before. I had puzzled over it by night, but forgotten it during the day.

Not this time. Today I was going to solve this little mystery, if nothing else. I would find the source of the mysterious light on the ridge.

Hustling into my clothes, I made a cup of tea and trudged down the hill to the barn. The October air was fine and clear, goldfinches sang their plaintive descending melody in the brush, Cinders the barn cat ran to meet me. Henry, Plumber, and Sunny all nickered eagerly. I smiled, fed the cat, and grabbed flakes of hay for each horse and dumped them in the feeders, checking to be sure the water troughs were full. Then I fed the banty chickens and let them out of the coop.

Another lovely autumn day. Just right for a hike in the woods.

Mac was instantly enthusiastic at my plan; Blue not so much.

"Can we go see where you found the body?" my son asked.

I was prepared for this; I'd known Mac would need to investigate this turn of events in his own way.

Ignoring Blue's look, I said, "Yes, we can go sort of near there. I don't think the cops will want us to go too close. But I can explain to you how it was."

"Good," Mac said, and I saw that though he hadn't mentioned it, the body in the woods had been on his mind. Best we face it directly.

"And I want to find the mystery light," I added.

"Can you see it now?" Blue asked.

I went to my spot by the hall window and peered. In full daylight it was hard to see but if you knew where to look it was still there.

"Yep," I said. "Come see."

Blue and Mac observed and concurred. We all agreed that it looked like it was on the ridge trail and yet there was nothing on that trail to cause it.

"We'll find out, Mama." Mac was obviously ready for this new adventure.

In an hour, after breakfast, we strolled down our driveway, Freckles on her leash. The autumn sunlight cast crisp, cool shadows and the air smelled sweet. Despite yesterday's events, I felt my spirits rising at the thought of a walk in the woods.

We crossed the busy road at the foot of our driveway, taking our time. Then we were plunging into the tangled woods, pushing through scattered strands of poison oak that reached out to grab us, seeing the openness and light of the first small meadow glowing through the oak tree trunks and rambling vines. Mac led the way; I followed; Blue and the dog brought up the rear.

The earth was damp and soft; Sunny's hoofprints were fresh and unmistakable—this was the way I'd ridden home yesterday evening. Now that I was so much nearer the ground, I could also see the prints of deer and what looked like a coyote, judging by both prints and scat.

Sure enough, as we entered the small meadow, motion at the far side of the clearing drew my eye. Mac had already halted. "Look, Mama," he said softly.

A slender young coyote glanced back at us as he melted into

the forest. Just a moment of grayish-brown dog shape, long pointed muzzle, pricked ears, turning and leaving. By the time Blue reached us, the creature had vanished. Freckles, grown increasingly deaf and short-sighted with age, did not seem to be aware that the coyote was nearby. I wondered if it was the pup I'd seen last summer, and silently wished him luck. Life could be very hard on yearling coyotes.

We trudged on up the hill, into the oak trees, shadows barring and dappling the trail. My mind wandered, thinking of the coyote, how he had simply appeared in the clearing. That was the thing about wild animals. These hills were full of them—deer, coyotes, bobcats, even cougars. And yet one went along and saw nothing. And then, in a moment, sitting on the porch, walking down the drive, hiking across a meadow, a shape appeared, and suddenly one was face to face with the wild. It was endlessly magical, constantly engrossing. And despite how often it happened, always unexpected.

The hill was getting steeper, and I paused to catch my breath. Mac charged ahead, eager to get to the top of the slope, where we might see the ridgeline and perhaps spot the mystery light. I could see his silhouette above me, striding along through the shadows. Mac could easily outhike me these days, and again my mind whispered nostalgically of the many times we had hiked in these woods when he was younger. Times when he was a very little boy.

An image leaped into my mind—not so many years ago, coming down the logging road one sunny winter afternoon. In my mind I see a young boy hiking down a green hill in brilliant sunshine. The boy is skipping and running more than hiking; he follows the old roadbed, leading west toward the bright light of the afternoon sun, which illuminates the new grass around us in a blaze of golden green. Papa and dog follow the boy; I am last, trudging down the hill, out of breath from the climb to the Lookout. The figures ahead of me are dark silhouettes against the thrilling sharpness of the winter light.

For that one moment I take it all in. The happy prancing boy, the complete family unit, the lovely shining California winter afternoon. My eyes lift and I can see the distant, tiny, triangular shape of our porch roof gable, far away on the opposite ridge. We are hiking the hills of home.

In that moment I am aware of how happy I am. I hope I can hold the image forever, though I know, as time passes, I may forget. But for now, I do hold the picture bright in my mind, crystal clear, a moment of pure and perfect joy.

"Come on, Mama." Mac's voice breaks into my reverie; he is looking down at me from further up the slope. "Come on."

I smile back at him and am aware that despite the yellow tape ahead, cordoning off the spot where Jane Kelly was shot, I am happy now, hiking with Blue and Mac. Nothing holds still, everything passes. For now, we remain.

Taking a deep breath, I plod on up the slope. Mac is waiting for me at the top and together we gaze through the screen of tangled scrub at the ridge across the valley, where we both know the ridge trail, and the mysterious light, are located. But we can see nothing unusual. Eucalyptus tree crowns rise in the morning sky, their tall, slender, pale trunks outlined against the shadows beneath them. No artificial light sparkles anywhere.

My eyes drop to the valley beneath us. Here, through the tangle of vines and bushes that screen us, I can see the paved suburban drive called Storybook Road. Along the road are perhaps a dozen large houses, all newish, all landscaped, all to my mind similarly ugly. Blue and I call them McMansions. This is the subdivision that was built in what was once a lovely meadow, not all that many years ago.

Mac follows my eyes and I raise a finger to my lips. He nods. We both know the rule. We don't speak to each other unnecessarily as we ride or hike near the subdivision. I had never forgotten the time that I had followed the old, much used trail along the pristinely paved road and been run off with many threats of invoking the sheriff's department by one of the new residents.

I could still remember the middle-aged man's face, contorted with rage, as he bellowed, "I told you damn horse people to stay away. You can't ride here anymore. I'll have the sheriffs on you!"

Fortunately, Mac had not been with me. But since then, I had used the little sidehill trail we were now hiking to avoid the subdivision and its hostile residents, and I had taught Mac to be quiet as we skirted the big houses. No doubt the inmates were all inside viewing some sort of electronic device, and we would not be visible to any but a skilled eye as we slipped through the brush, but still, there was no use making trouble we did not need to have. And some of the pet dogs had sharper eyes and ears than the owners.

We tromped on through the speckled shadows and flecks of dappled sunlight, moving silently through the woods, glancing from time to time at the opposite ridge, trying to spot the mystery light. No dice. Nothing there but trees.

Eventually we topped the ridge we were hiking and dropped over onto the other side. We were past the houses of the subdivision now, and rapidly approaching the spot we called the warm meadow. Mac moved steadily along ahead of me with a swinging stride and I had to trot to catch up with him. I tapped his shoulder and said softly, "Wait a minute."

Obediently, Mac halted, and in another moment Blue and Freckles were beside us. We stood in a little group, staring down across the sloping golden meadow, dotted with wild asters and baby's breath, warm in the sunny autumn morning. We could all see the strip of bright yellow at the bottom of the hill. We all knew what it was.

"Can we go down there?" Mac asked.

"It's got crime scene tape around it," I said unnecessarily. I was thinking of Jane's sightless eyes and the red hole in her chest.

"I doubt anyone's there," Blue said calmly. "The cops don't have enough resources these days to post guards on a crime scene like this. If we don't touch anything, we should be fine."

"Let's go." Mac was already striding down the slope.

I followed him, reassuring myself that the body was gone. At the most all we would see was some trampled ground.

This proved to be the case. We passed the spot where the four single-track trails met, and as we approached the pine tree that I'd tethered Dolly to, I could see that the crime scene tape encircled a small area of ground that looked as though many feet had trodden there recently. That was all there was to see.

"Her body was there." I pointed, in answer to Mac's inquiring glance.

"Somebody shot her," he said quietly, staring at the spot. "While she was riding her horse. I wonder why."

Silence greeted this remark. I imagined we were all wondering why. Was it some issue from her personal life, come back to haunt her with a vengeance? I thought of Sheryl Silverman, riding through the woods with black anger in her face and shivered. People did kill each other over stolen boyfriends or spouses. It happened all the time. Hard as it was to believe, it was a fairly common motive for murder. I decided not to discuss this with Mac.

"Can we go?" I asked plaintively.

Blue and Mac both glanced my way and then looked at each other.

"Let's go find the mystery light, Mama," Mac said.

Walking on past the yellow tape, we hiked across the warm meadow, not talking. We all knew that only perhaps a hundred yards away on our right lay the massive houses of the subdivision, screened as they were by trees. No use alerting any dogs or people to our presence.

Slowly the warm meadow narrowed, became choked by willows and scrub, as it approached a steep north slope ahead. The trail passed a dry hollow where a pond of peepers would shrill in the spring, and skirted a stony streambed which would then be filled with running water. We moved into the shadow of the ridge and the temperature seemed to drop at least ten degrees. I could feel the chill against my face. The willows closed in overhead and we marched through a tunnel of greenery.

"We're in the cold valley now," Mac said softly. He'd been hiking and riding these trails for many years. Like me, he knew every inch of them.

The trail started up the hill, entering a grove of redwoods. I stopped to rest, out of breath, and spotted a bright yellow banana slug, creeping through the dark brown redwood duff. I bent to peer at it. Banana slugs were not unusual, but all of the wild creatures were interesting, large and small. That was the thing about hiking as opposed to riding. One noticed so many more little things.

I looked up. Mac had halted and was waiting for me. Blue and the dog were just behind me, also waiting.

"I found a banana slug," I said.

"You're not fooling us, Mama, " Mac said. "We know you just need to catch your breath."

"True," I agreed. "There is a banana slug, though. Don't step on it," I added to Blue.

On we went, ever upward through the red-brown pillars of the redwoods, hiking in deep shade. I began puffing in earnest as I trudged. This hill was much more fun on horseback.

We emerged from the redwood grove into a leafy green tangle of wild currant and berry vines, rambling between the curving shapes of live oak trees. I followed Mac's form as he hiked relentlessly on. Up, up, up.

More light ahead of us indicated we had almost reached the three-way trail crossing, which marked the top of the slope. I pushed hard, eager to get there, hoping that we'd rest at that point, as we often did.

Sure enough, when I reached the flat at the top of the climb, which was dominated by a huge, multi-trunked, widely branching oak, Mac had halted and was waiting. I stopped beside him, and in another moment Blue and Freckles were beside me.

"Can we rest?" I asked, aware that I was panting.

"Sure," Blue answered. "Anyone want a drink of water? I've got some in my pack." Blue always hiked with a small daypack.

We all took a drink, including Freckles. I gazed around, remembering the last time I'd been here. Sunny and I had loped up that hill I'd just sweated my way up, and I'd paused here to try to call on my cell phone. And down the ridge trail had come a man with a yellow Lab and a machete.

I stared at the spot where I'd seen him. Halfway down that little hill. He'd met my eyes. I had no sense of what he was thinking. The machete had looked vaguely ominous, but realistically, he was probably using it to clear berry vines and poison oak from the trail, and away from his shorts-clad legs. The yellow Lab had wagged his tail in a friendly fashion, as is the way of yellow Labs. I had not a clue if he had any connection to Jane's murder.

"What about the light, Mama?" Mac's voice interrupted my train of thought.

"We need to go down the ridge trail a way," I said, "until we're at the place it seems to be coming from. Down in the eucalyptus."

"Let's go," Blue said.

On we went. Up the hill where I'd seen the hiker yesterday. I found what I thought were his bootprints in the dust, neatly superimposed on many horse hoofprints. I wasn't sure what good this was. As I hiked along, I would spot his track, then lose it, then spot it again. The man had clearly been coming down the ridge trail.

We entered a grove of big Monterey pines, some of them tipped over to make big stumps. Off to our right I could see a faint trail that led down to the landmark tree. I kept hiking, following Mac. From time to time I looked down at the dusty trail, but I no longer spotted the hiker's footprints. Lots of horse hoofprints, the occasional deer. Mac's very fresh footprints. That was it.

We were in the eucalyptus forest now. When Mac was a very small child he'd christened this the "Five Thousand Eucalyptus Tree Forest," in honor, I always supposed, of the Hundred Acre Wood in *Winnie-the-Pooh*. Anyway, like many of our names, it had stuck, and we always referred to this section in this way.

The eucalyptus trees were light and airy, compared to redwoods or oaks. They were slender, towering high, moving in the slightest breeze. Light slanted between them; the ground was carpeted with long shreds of their pinkish, peeling bark, dried lance-like yellow leaves, and their small hard blue cones. We tramped along, going mostly downhill now, following the spine of the ridge.

And there, not too many feet ahead, was the wide spot in the trail where I'd stopped and visited with Jane Kelly, not twenty-four hours ago. I stared at the ground as we walked by, not willing to bring this up to Mac or Blue.

A few minutes later we passed a trail that led off to the left, downhill, through the eucalyptus. Mac glanced that way, but kept on down the ridge. He knew the spot we were aiming for. And he, like me, knew where that trail to the left went. We'd ridden and hiked it many times. It was the way I'd come up yesterday on Sunny.

Up one more hill, and now we were coming down the steep part of the ridge trail. There was much more exposure, and big views opened up to the west. Down below us on the left was a group of houses—to the right, and east, was tangled shrubbery. We slithered on down the steep trail until suddenly Mac stopped.

"Look," he pointed.

I looked past him to see a tree across the trail up ahead. Not a huge tree. A smallish eucalyptus, lying across the trail about chest high to a horse. A very effective barrier to a mounted horseman. Too high and brushy to step or jump over, especially on this steep bit of trail.

I walked up beside Mac and looked at the tree. It had not fallen in this position, that was easy to see. It had been placed here.

Mac looked at me. "Somebody trying to block the trail?" he said questioningly. Like me, he'd seen this before.

"It looks like it," I said.

"Why do they do this?" he asked.

"Some people don't like horses," I said briefly. "Fortunately, since we're on foot we'll have no trouble getting around it."

Blue was beside us now, and he shrugged one shoulder. "Why don't we just clear it?"

"Can we?" I asked.

"Sure. Someone put it there. We can move it."

Freckles lay down on the trail, happy to rest, as Blue and Mac moved towards the tree. Between them, tugging and dragging, the eucalyptus was shifted and summarily pushed off the side of the bank.

"Good job," I said. Inwardly my mind was racing. I had wondered why Jane had apparently backtracked and now I thought I knew. She had come down the ridge trail, met this tree, and turned around and headed back. At a guess, she had retraced her way to the three-way trail crossing, headed down to the warm meadow, with the probable intention of riding up through the pampas grass meadow to the swingset trail and back to Moon Valley. But she hadn't made it. Her life had ended in the warm meadow...where someone had shot her.

Mac interrupted my thoughts. "Mama, shouldn't that light be somewhere around here?"

We'd descended a ways down the ridge trail. The houses on our left were now fairly nearby and just below us. "Yeah," I said slowly, staring that way. Blue was looking at the houses, too.

"Those houses," I said. Mac was staring at them, too.

The houses were actually below the trail, hidden behind the ridge from our house. We could not see them from our porch. We had never previously seen their lights.

"Look," Mac said, and pointed.

The nearest house, a tall three-story A-frame, had signs of fresh carpentry near the peak of its roof, as if someone had put in a loft or an attic. There was a small window that looked new. And in that window sparkled a bright little light. A brighter than normal light.

"I think that's a grow light," Blue said mildly.

Mac said, "I think there's a line of sight between that light and our house."

Standing on the trail, Mac sighted back in the direction of our house on the opposite ridge. Sure enough, we could all make out the shape of our porch gable through a screen of trees. Pointing at our house with one arm, he stretched his other arm to point at the light in the A-frame window. Definitely a line of sight.

"You're right," I said. "I think we've found the mystery light. And because of the trees we can only see it from certain places—like that window in the hall."

Mac had a big grin, and I knew he was feeling successful at having solved the mystery. I had other thoughts on my mind.

"I think that's the house that Ross Hart is renting," I said quietly to Blue. "That young guy who's training at the Red Barn. He's been there about six months."

"And I think he's built a loft and installed a grow light, don't you?" Blue smiled.

Neither one of us bothered to discuss why. We both knew. In Santa Cruz County indoor pot growing schemes were common. No reason for us to mention this to our eleven-year-old son.

I was remembering that Jane had said Ross was "up to some stuff he shouldn't be up to." Did growing pot qualify? Had Jane threatened to blow the whistle on Ross? Was I looking at a motive for murder here?

"We found it." Mac was still grinning. "Okay, I'm hungry, let's go home."

"Yes, let's go," I agreed, giving the lighted window one last glance. Was Ross Hart blocking these trails to keep people away so they wouldn't notice the light in his attic? I was willing to bet it wasn't visible from ground level by the houses.

As I hiked down the hill through the eucalyptus, my mind seethed with questions. I was going to have to talk to Jeri Ward.

*C*hapter 8

AN HOUR LATER WE'D RETURNED home from the hike and had lunch. I wandered down to my comfortable chair in the barnyard, pondering things. After awhile, I just watch the horses. All three of them look content, standing in the shade of the oak trees, apparently dozing. Occasionally a tail switches, a foot stamps, or a muzzle swings around to brush a side. There are always flies. But the horses don't seem to mind.

Sitting here, watching my horses, I am content. The puzzles and concerns of the morning seem to evaporate, and I just watch. Now and then my mind prods me, asking if I shouldn't do something, saddle Sunny, take Henry for a walk. But something else tells me to just sit and watch.

The horses are endlessly soothing. Watching them, for me, is what I suppose watching the sea might be for others. I stare idly and wonder what is it about these big livestock animals that I like so much. Having horses makes me feel connected to the natural world. Connected and empowered. I do not need to ride them to feel this. I just need to have them here, to care for them, tend them and be with them.

My eyes move across the little patch of rough grass where I let the horses graze to the grove of live oaks on the other side of the barnyard. Mac is flying through the air in a steady pendulum, rising and falling in his swing that hangs from a branch of the biggest tree. Mac's hair flares in the wind; Sunny walks over and stands close to the airborne boy. Sunny has seen this many times: he still likes to watch.

I see my son and the horse, together in the sunshine, amongst the live oaks, and I know, for one brief second, that more than anything else, this is the gift I am bringing to my child. Just being here with the horses, being part of each other's lives. Riding is wonderful, and we have done a lot of it, but being a family with our horses is more than riding them.

My eyes rest on Henry, who is snuffling the ground, looking for acorns. We'll be able to start riding him soon. But we are grateful simply that he is here with us. I smile at the sight of his bright eyes and cheerful white striped face. His sorrel coat gleams red in the sunlight with a glint like a shiny copper penny. Henry, our good horse, is still with us. The greatest gift is present now, as we are here in the barnyard together.

I resist the urge to move, to do. I sit and watch. And gradually my mind quiets. I know how fortunate I am. Every fiber of my being basks.

Ten minutes later the peace is broken. I see a car pull up by our front gate; I see the driver get out to open the gate and climb back in. I know who it is. Jeri Ward.

Almost instantly, my tranquil, meditative mood vanishes. The questions of this morning come bubbling back up in my mind. Sighing, I get to my feet.

"Who's that?" Mac asked.

"Jeri Ward, the detective who's investigating this shooting. I need to talk to her. I'm going to take her over to the little house, sweetie. We need to be private."

Mac took this in and then said, "I'll go find Papa."

I met Jeri as she parked her car. "Come on up to the little house," I said. "I've got some stuff to tell you."

Once we were seated, I said, "What happened with that young guy that your people picked up?"

"We arrested him on probable cause," Jeri said. "I think it's a mistake, but what could I do? There he was, not half a mile from the crime scene, hiking through the woods carrying a twenty-two rifle, and he wouldn't say what he was doing there. So, we took him in. I imagine he was probably trying to poach a deer."

"Do you think she was shot with a rifle?" I asked.

"She was shot with a twenty-two," Jeri said. "We just did the autopsy and found the bullet. Don't know whether it was a pistol or rifle. Twenty-twos are odd that way," she added. "One of the guys is going to fire our poacher's rifle this afternoon. That should tell us whether the bullet came from his gun."

"And if it didn't?"

"Then we let him go and start over," Jeri said.

"I found out something this morning," I told her. And I recounted the story of the mysterious light on the ridge.

Jeri took this in. "Can you tell me where that house is?" she asked.

I gave directions and Jeri took them down. Then she sat there, staring at the notepad in her lap. "I was going to ask you to draw me a map," she said, "showing where you met Jane, and how that relates to where the body was found, and where, exactly, you ran into the other folks that you mentioned. And I'd still like you to do that. But I just had an idea. What if I haul Gray Dog over here tomorrow, and we retrace your ride. Then you could show me."

"Sure," I said. "But it can't be tomorrow. Tomorrow I'm riding with Lucy Conners in the vet truck."

"Are you going back to work?" Jeri asked curiously.

"I don't know," I admitted. "I'm thinking about it. I'm not sure what I'm going to do."

Jeri grinned. "That's funny, " she said. "I turned fifty this year. I'm thinking of retiring."

"I turned fifty this year, too," I said.

We looked at each other. "Kind of a landmark, isn't it?" Jeri asked. "I've been with the sheriff's department twenty-five years.

I can retire right now with good benefits. I'm really thinking about it."

I smiled. "Blue inherited an almond orchard from his dad. Turns out we don't have to work anymore if we don't want to. I just don't know what I want to do. I'm still studying on it."

Jeri grinned again. "Yeah, that turning fifty is something. I don't know about you, but I hit fifty and went through the change. It makes you think. Like what do I want to do with the rest of my life? I think maybe I want to travel. Maybe ride my horse more."

I stared at Jeri. "The change, yeah, me, too," I said slowly. "And yeah, it does make you think. I'm thinking I don't want to be so busy."

Jeri smiled sympathetically. "Unfortunately I've got a chore for you. Could you draw me a map, please? And then I've got to go. I need to drive up into the subdivision and question the neighbors. And I might just call on Ross Hart and," she looked down at her notes, "Tammi Martinez."

I looked at the piece of paper she'd handed me. "Making you a decent map is going to take some time. Do you want to drop back by here after you've done your interviews?"

"Sure." Jeri got up briskly. "I'll see you sometime around five." And she let herself out the door.

I stared at the paper on the table in front of me as she drove away. I could see Blue and Mac down in the vegetable garden, harvesting dried beans from the scarlet runner vine, which was draped all over a bamboo tepee. I dropped my eyes, picked up the pencil, and began to draw the ridge trail.

An hour later I had a map. There was the ridge trail, with its neighboring houses; there was the eucalyptus forest and the landmark tree, the trail to the Lookout, the pretty trail, and the pampas grass meadow. There, too, was the warm meadow and the cold valley, the logging road and the swingset trail. I had marked the place where I met Jane and the place I found her body. I'd also marked the places where I'd seen Sheryl Silverman, Jonah Wakefield, the dirt bike, the mystery rider, the camper, and the hiker with his dog. I had marked the spot where I was when I'd heard the shot. I'd indicated where the subdivision lay. I'd even marked the spot where the ridge trail was blocked with a tree, with a little note explaining that Blue and Mac had cleared it this morning. It was a pretty complete map. I'd left out only my little sidehill trail that skirted the subdivision. I was hoping to keep that a secret if I could.

Mac and Blue were no longer in the garden, and the sun was sinking lower over the ridgeline. I reckoned it was about four o'clock. The late light slanted into the little room I was in and I settled back in the wicker rocking chair and stared around gratefully. I loved this house in the late afternoon.

Leaf shadows flicker on the dusty orange plastered walls. Soon the sun will be behind the ridge. In this moment it lights up the long, arching, overhanging canes of the big rambler rose named Treasure Trove that drapes the front porch of the house. If I look out the window at the rose vine, the leaves are brilliantly illuminated, backlit into diamonds of vivid green stained glass. If I look at the sitting room wall, the leaf shadows dance and play, making gentle, intricate shade patterns on the soft, earthy clay. I cannot decide which view of the rambling rose is more beautiful: the lit-up canes or the shadows on the wall.

This little house continues to amaze me. Nobody knows better than I do how it got built. I spent every single day of its creation with Blue and the crew; I heard the hammers bang, the saws whine, the men shout and laugh and tease each other. I argued and discussed and agonized with Blue over every detail: no one knows as I do how the hand-scraped hickory plank floor was chosen, why the walls are plastered a faded terra cotta color, or how the willow twigs came to line the open-beam ceiling. Despite this, the house appears to me as if it has always been here, exactly as it is now. Every detail appears inevitable, intrinsic to the whole. Though I know how the house was made, exactly as any other house is made, I still believe it was more born, coming into the world just as it was meant to be. I see myself as its midwife, rather than its creator.

My eyes drift around the sitting room, taking in the small, elevated alcove, with a rough, peeling, red madrone trunk as its defining pillar. I know how the tree trunk came to be here. The madrone tree grew down in the horse corrals; for many years I admired it. But madrones don't like traffic around their feet. Eventually it died. When we came to build the house, Blue said the *tokonoma* traditionally had a pillar of unmilled, "found" wood. The madrone was chosen, cut down, and given the place of honor. How it came to be that every sinuous curve of its upright, graceful trunk fit the small alcove perfectly, linking raised floor to ceiling beam in a rough, joyful, rising flight of unpredictable loveliness, I couldn't say. Like the rest of the house, it seemed meant to be.

I rock the chair and look at the old desk and the cedar chest we inherited from Blue's parents, at the hand-painted scroll in the alcove that Blue brought home from Japan. I smile at the beaded bamboo curtain that leads to Mac's room. I love it all. Perhaps that's the bottom line. Nothing fancy. I love this little house that we built.

The light is dying now; the sun's long rays disappearing, turning to a diffuse glow. I sit and rock. I can see Jeri Ward's car coming up the driveway. Soon I am going to have to go back to the world of murder suspects. But for right now, I am happy.

Jeri walked to the door and I waved her in. "Here's your map," I said. "And I want to show you something."

I pointed to the spot on the map where I had noted the downed tree that Blue and Mac had shifted. "I didn't come this way yesterday," I said. And I pointed to the route I had used to get to the ridge trail. "I came this way. So I didn't see this tree that was blocking the trail. But I'm guessing it was there yesterday afternoon. Which would explain why Jane apparently backtracked up the ridge trail and ended up in the warm meadow. I think she turned around when she got to the tree and came this way." I pointed again on the map with my finger. "I'm guessing she was aiming to ride from there up to the pampas grass meadow and from there strike the swingset trail back to Moon Valley. But she never made it." I thought of Jane's sightless eyes and shivered.

"Anyway, Mac and Blue moved that tree this morning. I guess we never thought of it being evidence, just a nuisance. It was obviously put there by someone who was trying to block the trail to horses. And I guess I told you that Jane and I talked quite a bit about all these trail access problems and how someone, we don't know who, keeps trying to block the ridge trail. Anyway, I'm sure she saw red when she met that tree. It would have been very hard to move single-handedly, while you were trying to hold your horse with one hand."

Jeri nodded. "I see."

"I did wonder, after we saw what I thought was Ross Hart's indoor agriculture, if he might not be blocking the trail so no one could look right at the light in his obviously new little attic. Did you call on Ross?" I asked.

"I tried," Jeri said. "No one home. I just worked my way around the subdivision."

"Learn anything?"

"No, not really. No one heard anything or saw anything. No one remembers the shot. A couple of people said they hiked the trails. Most said they never went up there. It's as if they all live in their houses and cars."

"Doesn't surprise me," I admitted.

"Anyway," Jeri said, putting my map in a folder, "I'm going back down to the office to find out if the bullets from the poacher's gun match up. Then I need to question the folks at Lazy Valley Stable and the Red Barn. Can we plan on a trail ride this week?"

"Sure," I said.

And Jeri Ward let herself out the door and was gone.

Chapter 9

THE NEXT MORNING I WAS seated in the passenger seat of my old vet truck, while Lucy Conners drove us to her first call of the day. This was a horse with an eye which was halfway shut, not too far from my place.

"After that," Lucy said, "I've got to go to the Red Barn. Ross Hart has one he's trying to sell and the woman who's buying it wants me to do a vet check. Oh joy."

I took that in. I knew exactly what Lucy meant about vet checks being no fun. But I was also very curious to observe Ross Hart. Perhaps, just perhaps, I could sneak in a few questions.

Lucy shifted the diesel truck into a higher gear, and the sound took me back in an instant to the many, many times I had driven this pickup to a vet call. For ten straight years I had worked non-stop as a horse vet, driving from barn to barn in this very truck. The thought brought a strange emotion; I almost shivered. Nostalgia and what? Almost revulsion. I couldn't tease it out immediately.

Lucy turned on McDonald Road and then, very quickly, into a driveway. In another moment we were bumping our way to a small barn. I could see a few fenced paddocks. A man stood in front of the barn, clearly waiting for the vet to arrive. I had never been to this place before—it had been built since my days as a practicing vet—and yet it was all so familiar.

This was my job, this was what I had been trained to do, what I had practiced for so many years. Even as I followed Lucy and was introduced to the man, my mind was running at warp speed on a track of its own. This was something I knew how to do, this was my job.

Watching Lucy examine the gray horse with the half-shut eye, I was already noting what would happen next. First she would stain the eye, tranquilizing the horse if it was needed, and then scan the eye with her pocket light, looking for any injuries or scratches on the cornea. If none were present, she would administer some eye ointment that contained a mix of antibiotics and steroids and perhaps give the horse some Banamine. This was what I would do, anyway.

Lucy proceeded with the exam. The man was holding his horse quite competently; the horse was tolerating having his eye looked at. Nobody needed me. And in that second, I registered the other part of my emotion and named it.

Mixed with the sense of familiarity and nostalgia, the inner certainty that this was my job and I could do it, was almost a flavor of boredom. Been there, done that. I was remembering just how many times I'd driven up to a barn to work on a horse with a half-shut eye, or a colic, or a lameness. Some I could help, some I couldn't. And then there was the sadness and frustration when I dealt with horses (or owners) who could not be helped, due to a serious condition, lack of money, lack of intelligence, you name it. It was dawning on me that just about the time I'd quit to become a mom, I had been feeling pretty burned out on this job. Somehow I had forgotten that.

It looked as though the gray horse had a healthy cornea; Lucy was giving the owner instructions on doctoring the eye. I watched her talk, taking in the sincerity and warmth in her fine-boned, olive-skinned face, and I remembered this part of the job, too. It was essential to get along with the clients, even the difficult ones, or one wouldn't have a healthy practice for long. Vets were judged on their ability to be personable as well as their skill in equine medicine. I remembered the distaste I had begun to feel at having to constantly "sell myself" to people. I knew just how to do it, assume that demeanor of kind, competent, in-charge, sympathetic professional, but did I really WANT to do it anymore?

The owner of the gray horse appeared to be a perfectly pleasant individual, but certainly there were plenty of jerks in the horse world and I'd dealt with lots of them. Did I want to go back to this? When I didn't have to?

Lucy must have noticed my somewhat abstracted expression as I climbed back in the truck. She put the pickup in gear, headed down the driveway, and turned to me.

"Whatcha thinking, Gail? Are you ready to go back to work?"

"I don't know," I answered honestly. "I've got a lot of mixed emotions."

I stared at Lucy, whose eyes had gone back to the road. She was much younger than me, in her mid-thirties, and had been working for Santa Cruz Equine Practice for ten years now. A strikingly attractive woman, she had remained single, and as far as I knew, focused on her job.

"How's it working for you?" I asked. "Do you enjoy it?"

Lucy sighed. "Yes and no. Well, you know. I get sick of being called out in the middle of the night. I can get tired of the people. But I love horses and the job's never boring. And I need to make a living. If I were in your shoes and could choose if I wanted to work, I don't know what I'd do."

"Yeah," I said, "I'm really conflicted." I sighed. "Let's just see what today brings." I wondered whether I should tell Lucy about my finding Jane Kelly up in the woods. I had noticed a short article in the paper about the shooting, but there was no mention of my finding the body, though there was a statement that a man had been arrested on probable cause. Apparently Jeri had chosen to keep my name away from the press.

In any case, we were already nearing the Red Barn; there wasn't time to tell her now.

"What sort of horse are you vet checking?" I asked. "Do you know?"

"Oh yeah. The worst sort. An older gelding, said to be a babysitter. This woman wants him for a husband horse. I think the horse is twenty. How likely is it he'll pass a soundness exam?"

I shrugged. We both knew the score. Older horses could be great mounts for beginners, but it was very rare to find one that was completely without soundness issues. Prospective buyers wanted the horse to "pass" a vet check, which few older horses could honestly do. In the end, a vet had to pronounce on a gray area—was this horse sound enough to do the job the buyer needed—and how long was he likely to stay sound. This was actually an impossible question to answer, and I, like Lucy, had hated doing vet checks.

"Ross is not gonna be happy with me if I flunk his horse," Lucy said, with a head shake. "And Ross can be a real butthead."

"Is that right?" I'd only spoken to Ross Hart a few times; mostly as I was riding past the boarding stable. I really didn't know him at all. But he had always struck me as a pretty tough customer. Now, remembering his indoor gardening project, I wondered just exactly how tough he might actually be. Hardened-criminal tough? Willing-to-murder-someone tough?

Lucy turned into the drive of the Red Barn boarding stable. I could see Ross at the hitching rail in front of the big barn with a middle-aged woman at his side. Tied to the rail was a tallish bay gelding.

"Here we go," Lucy said.

I watched her climb out of the truck while putting a friendly, relaxed smile on her face.

Yes, indeed, I remembered that reaction. I found I was pasting just the same sort of smile on my own face. Here I am, your pleasant veterinarian. Inwardly, I shook my head. Did I really want this life back again?

Lucy greeted Ross and the woman and introduced me. Ross and

I made cordial mouth noises at each other. I shook the woman's hand. The whole time I tried to watch Ross, wondering if I was facing a killer.

Ross's face didn't reveal much. In his mid-twenties, he was strongly built, with a thick chest. He sported a goatee and his hair was cut very short, in what I took to be a popular style, since I saw it so often. I didn't actually think that it flattered anyone.

Certainly not Ross Hart. His somewhat heavy, fleshy face was not improved by the little goat beard and almost shaved head. His small eyes had a closed, guarded expression, and his mouth was hard. He looked me over without interest and turned to the middle-aged woman beside him, smiling as he untied the bay gelding from the rail.

"Ace, here, is just what you need for your husband," he said in a genial tone. "This horse has been packing beginners for years and he can sure pack one more. I've taken people all over these hills on this horse." And he waved his hand at the ridge behind us.

I glanced at Ace and thought that the fairly high-withered, swaybacked animal looked as if he might be near the end of his working life, but Ross's comment opened the door for a question I wanted to ask.

"Do you ride these trails much?" I asked innocently.

"Sure, when I have time," Ross said. 'Why do you ask?" And for the first time his eyes met mine with a certain keenness in them.

"I was riding back there Saturday," I said, "and I thought I saw you."

A long silence greeted this remark. Ross appeared to be studying me carefully. I had the impression he was weighing things up in his mind, uncertain how best to answer. "Did you?" he said at last.

"Well, I thought so," I said. "Jonah Wakefield said he'd seen you, so I guessed it was you I saw. Riding a sorrel horse, loping along up the swingset trail, in the late afternoon," I added.

Ross Hart very clearly looked as if he'd like to ask me what the hell business it was of mine, but was unsure of the wisdom of this course.

"Might have been me," he said finally. "I was up there not too long ago on a sorrel colt."

"This would be day before yesterday," I said. "The day Jane Kelly was shot back there," I added, and watched his face.

The eyes narrowed and the lips tightened, that was for sure. The middle-aged lady launched off on "how awful" it was and how she'd read about it in the paper and of course she knew Jane on account of Jane used to board here. Ross Hart said nothing. His eyes watched me in a very wary way.

The horse-buying woman was concluding that Jane had probably been shot by accident by someone who was after deer. I nodded and watched Ross. Ross watched me. Stalemate.

Finally Lucy interrupted, saying that she had several more calls this morning. Ross immediately began leading the bay gelding down to the dirt parking lot where Lucy liked to do soundness exams—the same place I'd always done them many years ago. I trailed after the little group, soundness the last thing on my mind.

Ross Hart had clearly been unwilling to admit he was out riding on the trails Saturday, and yet I thought he had been. Why would Jonah Wakefield lie? And Jane herself had said that she had seen Ross, and "if looks could kill, I'd be dead." And less than an hour later she had been dead.

Just as I was contemplating this, a somewhat harsh voice behind me brought me back to the present.

"That's a damn good old horse."

I turned to find myself face to face with Tammi Martinez, the current manager of the Red Barn. I blinked. I simply wasn't used to tattooed women in halter tops at nine in the morning on an October day. Now that I thought about it, I had never seen Tammi when she wasn't wearing some sort of skimpy top that bared either her shoulders or her midriff or both. In this case it was both. The top, or lack thereof, revealed several tattoos, which I guessed was the point, more or less. Why have the tattoos if no one could see them?

On the other hand, Tammi was not a particularly young woman—I guessed her age to be somewhere around forty. Certainly she was slender enough that the tight jeans and minimal top did not look totally incongruous, but they weren't entirely flattering, either. The phrase "mutton dressed up as lamb" came to mind.

Of course, I reminded myself, this was really sour grapes on my part. I was big-framed, with wide shoulders and hips, and the older I got the more pounds seemed to want to attach themselves to my sturdy framework. On top of this, I felt no need to flaunt myself as an object of desire to any males in the vicinity. Thus my sturdy cotton cargo pants, comfortable but not fashionable, and a loose linen T-shirt.

"Hey Gail," Tammi greeted me. "Are you back at work?"

I'd known Tammi in the peripheral way one knows veterinary clients and other local horse folk for many years. "Not yet," I said. "I'm just thinking about it. I'm riding with Lucy today, that's all."

Tammi narrowed her eyes at Lucy, who was watching Ace trot in a small circle. Even from a hundred feet away, I could see the slight bob of his head that indicated the horse was not entirely sound. I knew Tammi could see it, too.

"I damn sure hope Lucy does not talk Estelle out of buying that horse," Tammi said, in a low, fierce whisper. "Ross needs the money bad. We need the money."

"We?" I said on a questioning note.

Tammi seemed disposed to confide in me, why I didn't know. "Ross and I are renting that A-frame house up the road," she said. "Rent's due tomorrow and the landlord wants twenty-five hundred a month. Neither Ross or I make all that much money running this place and training horses. He needs to sell this horse to Estelle. That damn Lucy better not queer the pitch. That horse is perfect for what Estelle wants to do with him." I had the impression Tammi was hoping I might influence Lucy towards passing the horse.

My mind was running on a different track. Tammi and Ross were renting that house together. This was news to me. I had heard they were an item, but not that they were living together. Maybe the indoor gardening was a joint project—a way to supplement their income. I tried another question.

"Running a boarding stable must be tough in this economy. I heard you lost a client Saturday."

Tammi's eyes shot to mine. "You mean Jane?" she said, and I did not miss the suddenly wary tone in her voice. It reminded me of the look in Ross's eyes when I'd brought the subject up.

"Didn't Jane used to board here?" I asked innocently.

"Used to," Tammi said sharply. "Used to is right. She hauled her horse out of here last week. Took the mare to Lazy Valley is what I heard. She still owed us a month's board."

"Really?" I said, on a questioning note.

Tammi was quite apparently bubbling over with pent-up emotion. "That damn Jane was a pain in the butt. Don't tell anyone I said so now that she's dead. Always complaining about something. She thought she should be the trainer here, instead of Ross. She was always hassling him, too. She was nothing but a troublemaker." Tammi took a quick breath. "Of course, I'm sorry somebody shot her."

Tammi did not sound sorry at all. On the other hand, I reflected, it would be hard to collect a month's board from a dead woman. Tammi and/or Ross had no real motive to kill Jane. Unless, of course, Jane had discovered their agricultural project and threatened to blow the whistle on them. That might constitute a motive. And Ross had apparently been riding back there when Jane was shot.

Tammi seemed to realize she'd said too much. "I need to go turn horses out," she announced abruptly, and wheeled around and went back to the barn.

I meandered down the hill toward Lucy, Ross, and the potential horse buyer, who were grouped in a half circle, looking at the bay gelding. Ace stood with his head down, calm and quiet, waiting for his fate to be decided.

I felt sad as I watched the old horse. This was something I had grown to hate about the horse business. The way older horses who had done a good job their whole lives were treated as disposable sporting equipment, dumped when their working life was done, often ending up at the local auction yard, to be sold to kill buyers who shipped them to slaughter in Mexico and Canada, under horrific conditions. It just didn't bear thinking of. My own horse, Sunny, had been saved from just such a fate. But there were countless other horses out there, just as sweet, who went to a miserable end. I couldn't rescue them all. I hated it.

Did I even want to be around this anymore? I watched Lucy explain to the woman that Ace could probably pack her husband at the walk and trot; he had some arthritic issues, but most older horses did have some of these. There was no way to know how long he'd stay sound enough to ride. The woman looked doubtful. Ross offered to lower the price.

And no one, I reflected, was talking about what would happen when the horse wasn't ridable. Ross, I felt sure, would simply send poor Ace to the sale. Would this woman care enough for a horse she would have owned a few years at most to bear the expense of retiring him? Pretty doubtful.

I closed my eyes for a minute, not wanting to see the kind, quiet, stoic expression in the eyes of the bay horse. You can't, Gail, I told myself.

I currently supported three horses who were retired and turned out to pasture in the Sierra foothills, besides the three horses I kept at home. I simply could not afford any more old horses. How in the world, I wondered for the first time, could I go back to this job? I would bring home a horse a week.

The horse-buying woman said she needed to think about it. Lucy shook hands and turned away. I could hear Ross talking, saying he could arrange cheaper board if the woman wanted the horse as I followed Lucy back up the hill to the truck.

"Yuck," I said, once we were back in the cab and headed out the driveway.

"Yep," Lucy agreed. "I hate doing vet checks on old horses. Almost as much as I hate euthing horses."

Lucy's words brought yet another picture to my mind. Virtually the last call I'd made as a practicing vet. Shortly after midnight on New Year's Eve, a woman I knew pretty well; her yearling warmblood colt had gotten scared by fireworks and tried to jump out of his corral. He didn't make it. The woman had found him on the ground, having half impaled himself on a post. He was breathing but unresponsive. I still remembered the frantic phone call. I was pregnant at the time and staggering out of bed at one in the morning to head out to a dire emergency seemed almost more than my increasingly fragile emotional system and increasingly bulky physical self could stand.

I'd reached the colt within twenty minutes, when a brief exam had made it clear that he was checking out. The woman had not hesitated, asking me to put him out of his suffering. Both our eyes had filled with tears as I administered the kill shot. I knew very well that she had no children and had saved for two years to buy the expensive young warmblood; he was her baby. And now, due to a freak chance, she was losing him at what should have been the beginning of his life. Even though I knew better than to take vet calls personally, in my interesting condition, it was all too much. The next morning I'd announced to Jim, my boss, that I needed to take a break.

"Yeah," I said slowly, still lost in my train of thought. "Euthing horses is always sad. Even when it needs to happen."

"I always hope I'm doing some good by reducing the amount of suffering they go through," Lucy said.

"And you are," I said automatically. This was what I had told myself, too, while I was doing the job. And, often, it was true.

"So where are we off to now?" I asked.

"Lazy Valley," Lucy said. "Doug Martin has a horse that's come up lame."

"Doug Martin?" I knew I sounded surprised. "He was Jane Kelly's boyfriend."

"Was he? She was the woman who got shot, out trail riding, right?" Lucy asked. "I assume that was some kind of accident?"

"Nobody knows," I said. I decided not to mention that I had found the body. Somehow I just didn't want to chat about it. I did, however, want to talk to Doug Martin.

I watched the landscape move by outside the truck windows, and wondered just how Doug Martin would be taking Jane's death. They'd only recently reunited, apparently. And what about Sheryl Silverman? My shoulders twitched a little at the thought of her. I could not get the picture of Sheryl's furious face out of my mind.

Rolling hills, dotted with oaks and pines, slid by outside the pickup; part of my mind registered that this was my familiar ridge, that I rode and hiked all year long. Today, though, my thoughts were elsewhere. As Lucy made the turn into Lazy Valley's long driveway, I hardly looked at the dirt trail that came down the hill to join the pavement, even though I'd ridden that path many times. This was where the swingset trail emerged.

My eyes scanned the numerous barns and corrals that made up the Lazy Valley setup. This was a much bigger boarding stable than the Red Barn. They had perhaps a hundred horses.

Lucy drove without pausing through the various barns and shedrows and arenas and parked near the last sizable barn. I could see Doug Martin sitting on a bench in front of it. Two women were talking to him. Sheryl Silverman and another woman I knew slightly named Trish O'Hara. Trish was holding a black horse by the bridle reins. Lucy and I got out of the truck and went to join them.

I have to admit I stared at Doug Martin and Sheryl Silverman with outright curiosity. Doug was talking, his handsome, fine-featured face quite animated. From what I could hear it sounded as if he were assuring Sheryl and Trish that Jane's death was an accident, that the police had arrested "some guy who was trying to poach a deer."

Lucy greeted the group; I smiled and nodded and watched faces. Doug, I thought, must be at least ten years younger than Jane had been. I put Jane's age at roughly fifty, the same as me. Doug might be forty, or even younger. He was an attractive guy, who always seemed to have a different woman with him. His charm lay perhaps as much in his boyish, unaffected manners, as his regular, even features. At the moment he was giving the group of us a sad, but still charming smile.

Lucy had just expressed her sympathy about Jane. Doug shook his head. "I still can't believe it happened," he said. "She was my good gal; I depended on her. She was always there for me."

I noticed that Sheryl's mouth thinned to a hard line when Doug said this, but her lips instantly relaxed into a gentle pout when he looked her way. Hmm. Now this was interesting. It looked like Sheryl might be trying to get Doug back, now that Jane was out of the picture.

Sheryl wasn't looking at me; she barely seemed aware that I was there. Her gaze was fixed on Doug, her big eyes, carefully darkened with product, held a sympathetic, friendly expression, as Doug described how he was looking after Jane's horse, dogs, and home. I couldn't hold back a tiny one-shoulder twitch as I remembered the black anger in this same woman's face Saturday afternoon when I'd mentioned seeing Jane.

Trish said, "I was planning to go ride the trails this morning, but now I just don't know if I should go up there. Coal's really good about everything, and I always felt perfectly safe on my own, but not if somebody's going to shoot at us."

"I'm sure that was an accident," Sheryl broke in. "Nobody would do that on purpose. I'm not scared to ride up there."

Silence greeted this remark. After a minute Trish sighed and tightened her cinch. "I guess I'm headed out," she said. "Come on, Coalie."

Trish mounted and rode off; Doug got up and said quietly to Lucy, "I'll go get that horse. I think he's got an abscess."

Lucy followed Doug into the barn. And Sheryl and I were left face to face. I watched a string of half-hidden emotions play across her quite pretty features. "Did the cops talk to you yet?" was what she finally said.

"Yes," I said. "I found Jane's body."

"You did?" From the sound of her voice I could tell that this wasn't yet common knowledge. Well, it would be now. But I didn't see any point in lying about it.

"Did you tell them you saw me out riding?" Sheryl demanded.

"Of course I did. I was asked to describe everyone I met that afternoon."

"Oh." Sheryl was assimilating this. "I guess you didn't have a choice."

"No. I had to tell them exactly what I saw. It wasn't personal." I decided not to mention that I had spoken to Jane and heard the story of the Jane/Doug/Sheryl triangle. Best not to go there. "Have the cops questioned you yet?" I asked.

"No." Sheryl looked doubtful. "Will they? Haven't they arrested someone?"

"I think they'll question everyone who might have seen Jane," I said mildly. "Did you see her out riding Saturday?"

"No," Sheryl answered, a little too quickly. "You told me you'd seen her. That's the only reason I knew she was out there somewhere. I never saw her."

"Did you hear the shot?" I asked. "I did."

Sheryl's eyes narrowed and her chin lifted. It looked as though she was trying to decide how to answer this. "I might have," she said finally.

"I'd tell the cops the truth," I offered.

"I did hear a loud noise," Sheryl said. "Not too long after I saw you. I didn't think of it as a shot. Maybe a car backfiring down on the road."

"Where were you when you heard the noise?"

"Riding down through the eucalyptus trees, going toward the high school."

I thought about that. It made sense. If Sheryl had kept riding after I saw her, and was headed towards the high school aiming to take what we called the long, flat trail back to Lazy Valley, that might be about where she would be when the shot was fired. She would have been on the other side of the ridge from the gun, and it was quite possible it had not sounded so loud where she was. Perhaps she might have mistaken it for a backfire.

Sheryl was looking at me and I could see doubt written all over her face. She clearly wondered what I knew and wasn't game to ask. I saw her eyes shift to the middle distance and looked where she was looking. Juli Barnes and Jonah Wakefield were walking in our direction.

I glanced over my shoulder into the barn. Doug was holding a bay horse, while Lucy bent over its right front hoof, digging with her hoof knife at the sole. Looked like Doug was right and the horse had an abscess. Neither of them seemed to need my help. And I wanted to talk to Jonah Wakefield.

Juli, the barn owner, was a tall, slim woman in perhaps her forties with very long black hair, usually, as now, worn loose. She seemed to regard her hair as her signature piece, and certainly the sweep of wavy black mane was very striking. Her face was strong-featured, with heavy brows and a look of confidence. I did not know if she had inherited money or acquired it some other way, but she was wealthy enough to have bought this boarding stable and its three homes several years ago, and seemed to be quite free of financial problems in general. Her problems had more been confined to trainers, a not unusual situation in the horse business. Trainers had come and gone at Lazy Valley with great regularity.

Currently she had the young, very good-looking Jonah Wakefield, who could not train his way out of a paper bag, in most local horsemen's opinion. By all accounts Jonah was not merely Juli's trainer, but also her live-in lover. Perhaps his status as trainer was directly related to this.

Juli and Jonah approached us at a strolling gait. Both looked very relaxed, very in charge, barn owner and trainer surveying the grounds. Jonah wore the black Stetson hat, a white shirt, tight blue jeans, and leather chaps with fringe. I suppressed my smile at the thought that Jonah had donned his chaps for a stroll around the barn. After all, they made him look so trainerly. Remembering the black duster he had worn for a ride on the ridge, I waved my hand at the pair of them.

Putting on the most naïve expression I could manage, I smiled sweetly and said to Jonah, "Didn't I meet you out riding Saturday?"

Jonah's dark eyes shifted alertly to my face. I couldn't really see his mouth under the thick black mustache he sported, but I had the idea it tensed up. Jonah's reaction to my question seemed remarkably similar to Ross Hart's. Apparently nobody wanted to admit they'd been out riding when Jane Kelly was shot.

After a moment's study of my features, Jonah apparently recalled that he had, indeed, seen me. "You were riding a palomino gelding?"

"That's right. And you were riding a buckskin colt." A poorly behaved buckskin colt, I thought but didn't say. The last thing I wanted was to get into a discussion about horse training with Jonah Wakefield or Juli Barnes. I knew perfectly well I'd be treated to a lecture on the principles of natural horsemanship and I didn't think I had the patience to listen to that.

Like many traditional horsemen, I thought that the natural horsemanship movement featured a little bit of real knowledge that most competent horsemen already understood. The rest of it was gimmicks and games that seemed to me to be mostly a way to put money in the horse guru's pockets, and to duck the actual process of getting on the horse and riding it. And, as Jane Kelly had pointed out Saturday, many horses that were a product of this system seemed both cranky and not very well trained—at least to those of us who were not fans of natural horsemanship.

Jonah was watching me closely, and I tried very hard to put an admiring expression on my face. Jonah was used to middle-aged women who admired him; I didn't figure I'd have much trouble convincing him I was one of the herd.

"Did that shot spook your colt?"

"Shot?"

"I heard a shot right before I saw you. I think it was the shot that killed Jane Kelly."

Juli, Sheryl, and Jonah were all staring at me. I batted my eyes at Jonah, remembering perfectly well that he'd denied hearing the shot when I'd met him on the trail.

"I went and got Jane's horse Saturday night," Jonah said slowly. "I didn't know she'd been shot until I read it in the paper Sunday morning. And no, I didn't hear a shot. I was loping up the hill; I might not have noticed."

"Did you see Jane?" I asked.

"No," Jonah said.

"But you did tell me you saw Ross Hart."

"Yeah. He was galloping across the meadow where the dirt bike trails are."

I thought about that a minute. The location would fit with my seeing him a little later loping up the swingset trail.

"Was he riding a sorrel horse?" I asked.

"Yeah. Why?" Jonah was plainly wondering what business this was of mine.

"I saw someone on a sorrel horse later," I said. "Looked like they were riding in this direction. I wonder why Ross Hart would be riding here?"

"I never saw Ross," Juli Barnes interjected quickly. "And I was out in the arena, working a horse that afternoon. I saw Jonah ride in. I saw Sheryl. I would have noticed if Ross Hart had come down the trail."

Juli's tone sounded defensive, I thought. All three of them looked at me as if they wished the ground would open up and swallow me.

Sheryl flipped her blond braid over her shoulder and spoke to Juli and Jonah. "Gail found Jane's body," she said. "The cops have been talking to her, asking her who she saw out riding."

All eyes zipped back to me.

"Yes," I said sweetly. "Of course, I had to tell the truth. I suggest you all do the same."

Out of the corner of my eye I could see Lucy emerging from the barn. She glanced in my direction, as if wondering if she should join me. Quickly I turned and moved toward her, saying over my shoulder. "Got to go."

But as I walked toward the pickup, I could feel three sets of eyes boring into my back. And it seemed to me that this little visit to Lazy Valley had raised more questions than it had answered.

Chapter 10

AT FIVE O'CLOCK THAT EVENING I was home and sitting on my porch. Lucy had dropped me off on her way to an after-hours emergency near Watsonville. I'd apologized and told her that I'd had enough for one day. But that wasn't what I was thinking. I was thinking I'd had enough for one life.

I wasn't used to being so frantically busy all day, so bombarded by people and their needs and demands. Ten years of not working as a horse vet had rendered the average veterinarian's day both uncannily familiar and disturbingly strange. This was my life…once. Not anymore. I wasn't sure what my life was supposed to be now.

I stared off across my garden, seeing Sunny's bright gold shape dozing under an oak tree in his corral further down the slope. Taking a deep breath, I consciously relaxed my shoulders, and noticed that the busy chatter in my mind began to still. Could a life be about this?

I put my feet up on the bench and allowed my gaze to drift around. I could hear the bittersweet descending song of a goldfinch in the brush. Flaming red leaves clambering into a nearby elderberry bush were no doubt poison oak, always brilliant in the fall. A long, liquid, golden light slanted onto the ridgeline across the road, lighting it up like a romantic Maxfield Parrish landscape. I sat and watched and thought.

To the western eye there is no particular merit in sitting on the porch, idly gazing at the garden. To such a perspective there might be merit in tending the garden, but merely contemplating it? No. And yet, despite my very western background, and the steady, straight-ahead performance that had characterised my working life, it was this seemingly pointless contemplation that drew me.

I didn't call it meditation; I didn't think of it as a spiritual practice, or want to give it fancy names or forms. I just wanted to hold still and be, watch the world around me. Somehow, without really knowing how I got here, I found myself wanting to be less busy, less focused on doing. Impossible as it was to explain to others, I just wanted to sit on the porch, doing nothing much at all. Watching the sun set; watching the light change on the ridge. That this was the polar opposite of a return to life as a practicing vet, I was now being forced to acknowledge.

Damn. I took another deep breath, waiting for the rush of adrenaline that the thought of being a working vet had precipitated to ebb. I wondered what exactly it was that drew me now.

The answer came in a rush, with no hesitation. It was the endless engaging play of nature that spoke to me. Storms blowing in, chickadees harvesting sunflower seeds from the big drooping heads in the vegetable garden, a buck drinking from our pond, the leaves of the wild grape slowly turning crimson. Sitting on the porch or wandering through the increasingly wild tangles of my brushy garden, seeing what roses were in bloom, feeding the horses and the chickens and then just watching them eat—these were the things that drew me. Not accomplishing goals, not interacting in the busy outside world. Unfortunate as it sounded to a western ear, I wanted to be rather than do.

I still liked to ride, but I no longer had any interest in competing or training. I liked to wander the trails along the ridge, watching the black oak leaves light up in brilliant autumn gold. The familiar trails fascinated me in all seasons. The trails… Sitting up straighter, I focused my gaze on the landmark tree. The long series of vet calls this afternoon had driven Jane's murder and my recent visit to Lazy Valley out of my mind. Surely I had learned some things I ought to tell Jeri Ward.

Blue and Mac were off playing miniature golf, a recent obsession of Mac's. I'd begged off on the grounds of being exhausted. I ought to have at least an hour before they got back. I dug my cell phone out of my pocket and dialed Jeri.

She answered on the first ring, her voice brisk. "Jeri Ward here."

"Hi Jeri. This is Gail McCarthy." I hesitated. Suddenly calling Jeri didn't seem like such a bright idea. She was heading up a murder investigation; what had made me think my information was so important?

"I heard a few things today I thought you might be interested in," I said diffidently.

"I'm almost next door," Jeri said. "I'll come around and talk to you. Be there in ten minutes."

I hung up and heaved a sigh of relief. Jeri had sounded interested and friendly. At any rate she hadn't sounded as if I was out of place to call her.

It wasn't even ten minutes before her car pulled up my driveway. As if on cue, we met on the porch of the little house and took our familiar positions on the couch and rocking chair inside.

"Is the young poacher guy still under arrest?" I asked her.

"No. The bullets from his rifle were rim-fired. The bullet from the body is a center-fire. Not the same gun," Jeri said. "We let him go."

"Oh," I said. I thought a minute. "Are you treating this as if it was a murder?"

"At this point we don't know if it was a deliberate murder or an accidental death. Either way, it's a homicide. Somebody pulled that trigger. Somebody killed her. What things did you hear that I might be interested in?"

I explained about riding around with Lucy and visiting the Red Barn and Lazy Valley. I tried to recount the conversations I'd had as well as I could remember them. Jeri listened carefully.

"You're right," she said. "That's very interesting. I arrived to question these people this afternoon, but I couldn't manage to track all of them down. Doug Martin, Juli Barnes, and Sheryl Silverman were nowhere to be found. I did manage to talk to Jonah Wakefield and Ross Hart. Both admitted to being out riding that afternoon. Both said they'd seen the other. Neither admitted to hearing the shot or seeing Jane."

"I wonder where Ross Hart was riding to," I said. "He was loping up the swingset trail when I saw him. That leads to Lazy Valley. But he never showed up there, or so I gathered from what Juli said."

Jeri looked down at her notepad. "All he said was that he was exercising a colt who had too much go. So he was loping him through the hills."

"I guess he could have loped up the hill and come right back down. I wonder if he saw that dirt bike rider. Did you question him?"

"I'm not sure," Jeri said.

"I'll bet dollars to donuts he lives in that big fancy subdivision," I said.

"I talked to a young guy with a beard who said he sometimes went out on the trails," Jeri said. "He didn't mention a dirt bike. He lives with his parents in a big gray house that's about the third one up the street. Name's Leonard Harris. Calls himself Len."

"I bet that's the guy I saw," I said. "It was right after I heard the shot. After I saw Jonah Wakefield," I amended.

"The thing that interests me," Jeri said quietly, "is that Sheryl Silverman was making nice with Doug Martin. I find that very interesting. And Ms Silverman was neither at the barn or at her home when I went looking for her this afternoon. Nobody knew where she was."

"Doug basically said he was living at Jane's house," I offered. "Said he was taking care of the house and animals. But I have a feeling he was living at Jane's house before she was killed. Doug always seems to be living with some girlfriend or another. I noticed he tended to pick women who had a home. And I've never heard of him having a place of his own. I hate to say it, but I've wondered if he didn't take up with Jane again because of that. Jane was a solid citizen and owned a nice home in Rio del Mar. Sheryl rents a condo—or so I heard. Maybe Jane looked like a better deal."

"I wonder who inherits the house?" Jeri said meditatively. "In any case, Doug Martin and Sheryl Silverman are at the top of my need-to-question list, and I'd better get out there and look for them. Can we go on a trail ride tomorrow?"

"Sure," I said. "When?"

"I'll be here about eleven."

"Okay," I said. "I'll be ready."

And Jeri headed off down my driveway, just as Blue and Mac drove in.

Chapter 11

WHEN THE BEIGE PICKUP pulling an aluminum horse trailer arrived in my barnyard the next day, I was already saddling Sunny. I watched out of the corner of my eye as Jeri unloaded a tallish flea-bitten gray gelding. Sunny pricked his ears at the newcomer; Henry nickered a greeting. Jeri's horse looked around calmly; I noticed that she'd hauled him saddled.

Jeri's gear looked much like mine—a well-used western saddle complete with back cinch and breast collar. Mine was an old roping saddle, dating from the days when I used to compete on Gunner.

"Hi Jeri," I called, pulling the cinch tight on Sunny. "Ready to hit the trail?"

"Soon as I get him bridled." And Jeri took the bridle off the saddle horn and offered her horse the bit, which he took in a mannerly way. Looked like Gray Dog was a solid citizen.

I slipped a mechanical hackamore on Sunny, checked the cinch one more time, and climbed aboard. Jeri swung her leg over her horse and looked at me. "Let's go."

I led off down the driveway, Sunny walking slowly, as he usually did at the beginning of a ride. As we headed out through my front gate, Jeri asked, "Where's your kid today?"

"At school," I said. "He goes to a two day a week program for homeschooled kids. He loves it."

"How's homeschooling working out for you?" Jeri asked, as we rode between my neighbors' houses, headed for the road.

"It's been great," I told her. "Mac and I have stayed close, and he's become a really confident learner. He's made friends, and they've been totally positive relationships. He hasn't had to go through the sort of nasty social bullying that went on in my grade school, anyway."

"Mine, too," Jeri agreed. "That stuff really scars you."

"Well, as far as I can tell, Mac isn't scarred," I said. "He loves to learn, and he likes people and feels open to them. He's a happy kid." And I smiled.

"Good for you," Jeri said. "You followed your own path."

We reined our horses up by the side of the busy country road. "I'm going to cross here," I said, "and then cut across that parking lot and through the Red Barn boarding stable."

"I'll follow you," Jeri said.

We waited side by side for a gap in the traffic, then crossed the road at a brisk walk. Gray Dog, I was pleased to see, was as calm as Sunny.

Jeri saw my glance at her horse. "He's a good boy," she said. "Nothing much bothers him. He's seventeen this year, and since he used to be both a team roping horse and a ranch horse, he's seen a lot of stuff. I was lucky to get him."

As we rode up the dirt road that led through the boarding stable and on toward the ridge, I glanced automatically around. A woman was schooling a horse in the arena; two girls were cleaning pens. No one I knew. Ross and Tammi were nowhere to be seen.

"I'm taking you the way that I rode on Saturday, when I found Jane," I told Jeri.

"Did you see anyone in particular when you rode through here?" Jeri asked.

"Not that I remember," I said. "I think there were a few people around, like there are now, but no one I recognized."

I glanced at the A-frame house at the end of the road as I took the trail that led off to the right. All quiet. Maybe Ross and Tammi were inside, having lunch.

Sunny marched confidently along the trail, which rolled up and down over little hills, past big pine snags, and through a grove of feathery acacia trees. We stepped over a fallen log, and ducked for a low branch. I looked back to see Jeri following suit. As we emerged from the acacia trees, my gaze shot up the hill to a blue house that was clearly visible from the trail. A furious volley of barks announced approaching trouble.

"Hang on," I said tersely to Jeri, "that is, if he's afraid of dogs."

Jeri grinned. "He doesn't like dogs," she said, "but he's not afraid of them. He might kick one. He attacks dogs."

"Don't let him, if you can help it. We don't need trouble from this guy."

The big white dog, who looked like a standard poodle, raced down the hill toward our horses, barking the whole time. I could see the owner clearly, standing in the driveway, making no attempt to call the dog off. In fact, I was pretty sure he'd sicced the dog on the horses.

The white dog dashed around us, yapping and pretending to nip. I kept a steady pace down the trail; Sunny ignored the dog. Gray Dog pinned his ears, but Jeri kept him on a tight rein and he did not lash out at the diving, darting dog.

"What's the deal with that?" Jeri said, as we passed the house and the dog returned to the driveway.

"That guy doesn't like the horses riding through here, or so I've heard. But he can't stop us; the trail's not on his property. So he sics the dog on people. It's one of the things Jane said she was upset about when I saw her."

Jeri and I looked back to see the distant man staring at us, his pose and gaze obviously defiant.

"Nice guy," Jeri muttered. "Think I'll call on him and find out his whereabouts when Jane Kelly was murdered."

"Good idea. I didn't see either him or his dog when I rode through here Saturday afternoon."

Laura Crum

I took the left-hand trail that led up through the Five Thousand Eucalyptus Forest, following the route I'd taken then. Though only a couple of days ago, it seemed like eons of time had passed, so much had happened. The eucalyptus forest was unchanged; the tall, pinkish, peeling trunks swaying slightly in an infinitesimal breeze. Shadows dappled the trail and leaves crunched under the horses' hooves. Sunny clambered steadily as the route grew steeper, stepping over fallen branches, following the trail as it wound between the slender trunks.

When we reached the spot where this trail joined the ridge trail, I turned right and indicated a wide place up ahead. "That's where I met Jane," I said.

"How did she seem?" Jeri asked. "Calm, upset?"

"Normal, for Jane. Friendly, feisty. Jane was kind of a feisty personality. We got started talking about trail access problems and she was upset about that guy with the white dog. And the dirt bike guy. And whoever it is that's been blocking the ridge trail. Not to mention her various boarding stable dramas I told you about. All that was typical of Jane."

Jeri said nothing to this, just looked carefully at the spot. "I know which way you went from your map," she said finally, as we continued up the trail. "Which way do you think Jane went?"

"I think she went down the ridge trail until she came to the tree that was blocking it. That's the way she was headed, anyway. And then I guess she came back up this trail and turned left at the next junction. It would make sense, considering where she was found."

"Let's go that way," Jeri said.

We rode steadily, leaving the eucalyptus forest for the grove of big Monterey pines. Jeri indicated a faint trail that led off to the left. "Where does that go? Is that the trail you mean?"

"No," I said. "That goes down the hill towards the base of the big landmark tree, and from there it goes further down and ends up in that subdivision on Storybook Road. Horse people don't use it. I think only people from the subdivision that hike up here on the trails use it."

"Horses don't go down there?"

"No. The people in that subdivision don't like horses. They banned them."

"Oh," Jeri said.

We rode on until we reached the three-way trail crossing. I pulled up on the flat under the oak tree, and pointed at the trail that led to the Lookout and the pretty trail. "That's the way I went on Saturday. And then I came back through here," I pointed at the left-hand trail, leading down the hill, "after I found Jane. I met the hiker with the dog right here, after I found Jane's body."

"Was he someone you'd seen before?"

"I'm not sure, " I said honestly. "I do see people out hiking with their dogs, and yellow Labs are a pretty popular breed these days. I might have seen this guy before. He looked kind of familiar. But I'm not sure. He was just a middle-aged man, kind of thick-looking, wearing hiking shorts and carrying a machete. I think the machete struck me as ominous at the time, but he was probably just using it to clear poison oak and brambles away from the trail."

"How did this guy seem? Upset, calm, friendly?"

"Hard to say. I was pretty upset myself. I remember meeting his eyes and wondering if I should ask him for help and just not knowing what to do. In the end I headed off to the Lookout because I knew my cell phone would work from there. I never spoke to him or him to me. I'm guessing he's somebody from the subdivision who comes up here to walk his dog."

"Okay. So let's go the way you think Jane went," Jeri said.

"Sure." And I led off down the hill through the tangled green shrubbery.

Sunny walked briskly, picking up the pace a little. Sunny knew perfectly well that we were now headed in the direction of home. Like most trail horses, Sunny walked a little more quickly on the way back. To his credit, he did not jig or prance in an annoying way. He just marched.

Down we went, through the blackberry vines and wild currant, detouring for a downed tree—the path well worn by many previous feet. In a minute or two we were in the dim shadows of the redwood grove, the red-brown trunks towering on both sides of the trail. No light sparks penetrated the thick canopy far above. A hushed chill seemed to fill the air.

"Brrr," Jeri said.

"Yeah, I know," I said, looking over my shoulder as I spoke so that Jeri could catch my words. "It's always cold here. We call the spot at the bottom of this hill the cold valley. It's usually at least ten degrees colder there than in the meadow where Jane was shot." I swallowed. "We call that place the warm meadow," I said, thinking that I very sincerely hoped that it didn't become the "place where Jane was shot" or "place where I found the body." I didn't want to think of it that way.

The two horses reached the bottom of the slope and Sunny stepped confidently across the streambed at the bottom and along the trail that led to the warm meadow. Jeri and Gray Dog followed. Despite the nature of our errand, I couldn't help enjoying the bright autumn sunshine flickering between the green leaves of the willows and the fresh smell of the loamy ground under the horses' hooves. The very rhythm of Sunny's brisk walk made my heart lift.

We paced steadily out into the sunshine of the meadow; the light dazzled my eyes after the shadows beneath the trees. When I focused I could see the yellow crime scene tape and the scrubby pine tree where I'd tied Dolly. Jeri and I pulled our horses up. I stared somberly at the heavily trampled ground encircled by the tape.

"We never did find the spent cartridges," Jeri said.

"Does that mean something in particular?" I asked.

"Not necessarily. They're small and can be missed. But it could mean that the woman was shot from a distance, not up close, and that the cartridges just aren't here in this clearing. Which might indicate a twenty-two rifle, rather than a pistol, was the weapon."

I thought about that. "That would eliminate the people I saw," I said. "I don't think any of them had somewhere to conceal a rifle."

"Uh-huh," Jeri said. "And it tends to make the shooting look like either a true accident or very premeditated. Not some sort of confrontation on the trail and the shooter pulled out his gun."

Suddenly Sunny lifted his head and pricked his ears. I looked where he was looking, and my heart seemed to jump into my throat. Walking down the trail towards us was a man—carrying a rifle.

"Jeri," I said quietly.

Jeri's head turned; she saw what I saw. Her eyes narrowed as the man came walking toward us. The rifle was held loosely in his right hand, not pointing at anything. The man met our eyes and jerked his chin up in a minimal greeting. Jeri and I, and our two horses, watched him approach. My heart thumped a steady tattoo. I had no idea what, if anything, I should do. Jeri was a cop, a trained professional. I waited for her to give me a lead.

The guy looked like a young man, perhaps in his twenties. His blondish brown hair gleamed in the sunshine. He was strongly built, and despite his regular, even features, he did not bring to mind a pretty boy. This guy looked tough. His face was calm, neither friendly or unfriendly. When he was twenty feet away, Jeri spoke. "Hello, Brandon. Out for a walk in the woods?"

The man stopped. His eyes, even at this distance an obvious, brilliant blue, looked sharply at Jeri's face. "Sergeant Ward," he said slowly. "On a horse."

"That's right," Jeri said. "This is Brandon Carter," she added, looking briefly at me. "The man we picked up and released."

"Oh," I said.

Brandon Carter met my eyes. "After they determined it was not my gun that shot the woman." He looked back at Jeri. "I don't shoot women."

"So it appears," Jeri said mildly. "How come you're walking through the woods with a rifle in your hand?"

"No law against it," Brandon said. "There's mountain lions back here."

"True," I agreed. "I saw one once, out riding."

Brandon looked interested. "What did it do?"

"Disappeared into the brush."

Jeri shrugged one shoulder. "Brandon hasn't been willing to be too forthcoming about why he hikes around with his rifle in hand, which is mostly why he got picked up in the first place."

"No law against it," Brandon repeated.

"There's a law against firing it," Jeri said mildly. "In this county, anyway. You need to go to a range."

"I know that." Brandon folded his arms across his chest, cradling his rifle in the crook of his left elbow.

"So what are you doing out here today?" Jeri asked him.

Brandon considered that, arms crossed. "I don't like people shooting women up in the hills," he said at last. "I'm just having a look around."

"We don't need any vigilantes around here, Brandon," Jeri said.

"Did I say anything about being a vigilante? I'm just having a look around. I walk in these hills a lot."

"All right." Jeri's tone was cool. "And if you see anything worth mentioning, I'll thank you to let me know."

"Yep." Brandon looked her straight in the eyes. "I'll be sure and do that."

Jeri looked at me and gave an infinitesimal shrug. "Let's go," she said.

As we turned our horses, I looked back. Brandon still stood in the trail, arms crossed, rifle held in the crook of his arm, eyes watching us. "See you around," he said.

When we were out of earshot, I turned and caught Jeri's eye. "What's with him?" I asked.

"I'm not sure," she said. "He was pretty angry at being accused of this shooting."

I watched Sunny's yellow ears for a minute, then turned back to Jeri. "Why would he be angry?" I asked. "Surely he could see why you'd suspect him."

I could hear the shrug in Jeri's voice as she replied. "You'd be surprised. It's a common reaction. People are really offended at being accused of a crime they didn't commit."

"And you're sure that guy's innocent? He seemed to have an attitude."

"Yep. Brandon has an attitude. But that rifle didn't kill the woman."

"And it's really legal for him to carry it around like that?"

"Yep. Not legal for him to fire it, though."

We'd reached the trail crossing and I halted Sunny. "Which way do you want to go?" I asked Jeri.

"I'd like to ride the route Jane would probably have taken back to Lazy Valley," she said.

"That would be the swingset trail."

Jeri nodded. "But first I'd like to go check out the camper you saw."

"Didn't your people check on that already?" I asked.

"They found the camper. No one was around that evening, apparently. I went up there Sunday and yesterday and couldn't find a soul. But the camper was still there."

"Okay," I said, taking the narrow trail that led to the pampas grass meadow. "Let's go see if it's still there now."

Sunny walked slowly; he'd displayed an obvious reluctance to take the trail that led away from home, but I'd booted him and he'd acquiesced, with a decent amount of grace. Now he was walking out again, covering the country in a long swinging stride. We passed through the tangled greens of oak trees and manzanita and emerged into the openness of the big meadow, studded with feathery clumps of rustling pampas grass. We'd had a few early rains, so the loose ground wasn't too dusty, and Jeri and I rode along quietly through the bright air. I could see the skeleton shape of the landmark tree perched on the ridge to my right.

Once across the meadow, I reined Sunny to the left, up the logging road, a mere couple of ruts through the rough grass. Up we went, past a big pine snag, around a couple of bends, and there it was. Pulled off to the side of the road on an old log deck sat the battered camper. With a man standing beside it.

I looked back at Jeri, who nodded. Both of our eyes were fixed on the short, stocky form of the man, whose shaved head gleamed like a pinkish billiard ball in the sunlight. The guy had seen us and watched our approach. He grinned, what struck me as an oddly goofy expression. Somehow he gave me the creeps. I halted Sunny and Jeri rode by me, stepping closer to the man and his truck.

"Hello there," she called. "I'm Detective Jeri Ward of the Santa Cruz Sheriff's Department. I'd like to have a word with you, please."

"Sure." The man was still grinning. I one hundred percent for sure did not like his expression. "I'll talk to anyone," he said.

Jeri dismounted from Gray Dog and handed his reins to me. Taking a notepad and pencil from her pocket, she stepped nearer to the bald guy.

"Could I have your name?"

The grin remained in place. I swore I could see white all around the grayish iris of his eyes. "Buddy," he said.

"Buddy what?"

"Just Buddy. I'm like Cher. And Madonna. One name."

Jeri didn't flinch. "Your address?"

Buddy shrugged. "No address."

"Where do you live?" Jeri asked him.

"Here." And he patted the fender of the battered truck. I saw Jeri glance at the license plate and write the number down.

"Do you have permission to be parked here?"

He shrugged again. "Who would I ask?"

"How long have you been here?"

"A few days." Buddy's grin was fading a bit. He watched Jeri warily as she took notes.

"My friend Gail here saw your camper parked in this spot on Saturday afternoon."

"Is that right?" And Buddy's oddly round eyes fixed on me.

"Yes," I said. "I did see your camper here when I was riding."

"Must have been here then."

"Did you hear any shots that afternoon?"

"I can't recall." Now Buddy looked defiant.

I saw Jeri stoop down and pick up an object from the ground. Something small. "This looks like a cartridge from a twenty-two," she said. "You been doing any shooting here?"

"Not me." Buddy's tone was sullen and he looked at the ground.

Jeri walked to the edge of the bank. I followed her with my eyes. I knew we were both thinking the same thing. Was there a line of sight from this spot to the place where Jane was shot? It looked like there could be.

Jeri turned and glanced behind the camper. I could see the wheel of a mountain bike. "Is that your bike?" Jeri asked.

"Yes."

"Been riding it much?"

"Every day." Buddy was muttering now, looking down. In a barely audible tone he added, "Not that it's any business of yours."

Jeri glanced up at me. "All right then. We'll be going."

Taking Gray Dog's reins from me, she remounted. Buddy continued to look at the ground, ignoring us as we turned our horses and rode back down the hill. I did not look over my shoulder, but I could feel ripples of discomfort up and down my spine. I did not trust Buddy one little bit.

"That guy's not normal," I said, once we were around the bend and out of his sight.

"Yep. I need to talk to him some more. And I'll bet this cartridge came from his gun. As soon as we get done with this ride, I'm gonna grab one of the guys and come back up here."

Jeri and I were both silent as we took the trail that led to the swingset. "This is where I saw what I guess was Ross Hart," I said finally, as we came to the hill that led up through scattered oak trees to the crest of the ridge. "Loping along."

"Yeah," Jeri said absently. I could tell she was lost in her own thoughts. For that matter so was I.

And my thoughts were making me really uncomfortable. Talking to Buddy had caused me to think for the first time that Jane might have been shot not by accident, or for a reason, but for no reason. Somehow, previous to this, I had supposed that if she were murdered, it was by someone who had a motive to kill her. Not by someone who had simply and randomly chosen to shoot an unknown woman riding through the hills. Someone crazy.

The thought made my shoulders twitch. Almost involuntarily, I looked over my shoulder. The trail stretched, empty and quiet, behind Jeri and Gray Dog. No one there. Or so it appeared.

I thought of Jane Kelly riding her steady horse down the trail, as we were doing now, with no thought of danger. I thought of someone hidden in the woods, aiming the gun, pulling the trigger. For no particular reason, or no reason that would make sense to anyone else. I thought of Buddy. And for the first time since the shooting, I seriously wondered if I ought to be riding back here.

Jeri and I were out of the trees and in a small meadow, passing the abandoned swingset that had given this trail its name. I remembered another time that Sunny and I had galloped past this swingset on a stormy day and sincerely hoped I would not see a repeat of that event. Looking off to the left, I glanced at the remains of an old house, half buried in twining vinca. For a moment I pictured the children who had once lived in the house and played on the swingset.

Movement ahead of me in the dark woods caused me to look quickly back at the trail. The movement resolved itself into someone riding toward us through the shadows on a dark horse. As the horse and rider emerged from the trees, I recognized Trish O'Hara on her black gelding, Coal.

Trish pulled her horse up with a look of relief on her face. "Oh, it's you, Gail. I swear, I'm completely paranoid right now. Every time I see anyone I'm afraid it's the person who shot Jane."

"I know what you mean," I said. Gesturing at Jeri, I added, "This is Sergeant Jeri Ward, who's investigating the shooting. This is Trish O'Hara, Jeri. She keeps her horse at Lazy Valley."

"Nice to meet you," Trish said. "I think I saw you at the barn yesterday afternoon talking to Doug and Sheryl."

"That was me," Jeri agreed.

"Sheryl wasn't too happy about that," Trish said, and grinned. I got the idea that Trish's opinion of Sheryl was about like mine.

"Is that right?" Jeri asked in a friendly way.

Trish shrugged, but didn't say anything more. I wondered if I ought to warn her not to go near Buddy's camper. But then, I knew no real reason to speak ill of the guy. In the end, we wished each other a nice ride and went on, Jeri and I leaving the bright meadow for the shadows of the forest.

In another minute we were in the midst of a big grove of redwood trees, with views between their trunks all the way down the long valley. Beyond lay the crumpled folds of the coastal mountains, blue with distance. Sunny paced calmly on; Gray Dog followed. Through the scrub, and out into the sunshine again, with a view through the oak trees of the Monterey Bay.

"Wow," Jeri said. "This is sure beautiful."

"Yep," I agreed. "Even if we are working on an ugly crime."

The trail wound slowly down the hill toward Moon Valley. Some ten minutes later we were riding through Lazy Valley Stable. I glanced in the direction of the barn where Doug Martin kept his horse. There he was, with the bay gelding tied to the hitching rail. Doug was apparently rewrapping the foot with the abscess. Next to him stood Sheryl Silverman, holding her saddled mare by the bridle reins. She was talking to Doug and it seemed to me there was real intensity in her face and posture. I couldn't hear her words. Neither Doug nor Sheryl had noticed Jeri and me yet.

Doug's face was turned up toward Sheryl now; there was something there that I couldn't read. Not anger exactly, more like fear.

Doug's usually relaxed, handsome features definitely held an expression of alarm and yes, frustration. He answered Sheryl with the same intensity in his face and body language that I saw in hers. I glanced at Jeri and saw she was watching the two of them. In that moment Sheryl looked over her shoulder and spotted us. It was actually pretty comical. For a second we registered as just two riders walking down the dirt road that led through the stable. Sheryl's eyes narrowed as she focused closer and recognized me. But when she identified Jeri her jaw literally dropped and she turned instantly to Doug. Both of them watched us ride towards them with wide, startled eyes. Deer in the headlights.

To my surprise, Jeri smiled a greeting but kept on riding. I followed suit. As we rode out the gate at the other end of the ranch, I looked a question over my shoulder at her.

"I talked to those two yesterday. Didn't learn much. Sheryl admits to riding up in the woods during the time Jane was shot. She heard something that might have been a shot. Doug has no alibi. Says he was running errands. His horse is lame so he can't ride. And then he told me all about how he was taking care of Jane's home and animals. Very devoted guy, or so he says."

"Yeah, I wonder about that, too."

"I sure wish we could have heard what they were saying to each other back there. It was something more than trivial chat," Jeri said.

"That's what I thought, too. They looked pretty intense."

"So, where are we going now?" she asked me.

"Back to my place. We'll ride over this ridge here and then back across the high school. It's a nice ride."

Famous last words. We had only gone a short way up the steep slope, riding a narrow single-track trail that snaked between the trees and brush when, on a particularly vertical sidehill in the midst of tangled vines and bushes, we came to a downed tree. A recently fallen tree. Like maybe yesterday.

I stared at the trunk in consternation. A pretty good-sized oak, it lay across the trail in such a fashion that it was too high to step over and too low to duck under. The trail was effectively blocked.

"Is this another example of somebody trying to keep horses off the trails?" asked Jeri from behind me.

"I don't think so," I said. "This tree looks like it's tipped over naturally and it's too big for someone to place here. I think it's just an act of nature."

"So what do we do?"

"I'm not sure."

Sunny stood perfectly still as I studied the situation. The trail was narrow, the hill it traversed was steep, and the brush was thick. The path was completely blocked. I wasn't sure that we could turn around safely. I wondered if we could detour around the tree. It had fallen with its crown to the uphill side and the more I looked the more I thought that maybe we could detour around it. If our horses were willing to go straight up the hill while pushing through tangled bushes, vines, and small branches.

"How's your horse at bushwhacking?" I said over my shoulder to Jeri.

"He's fine," came the laconic answer.

"Okay then. Here we go." And I aimed Sunny straight up the hill and clucked to him.

My little yellow horse knew how to push through brush, and steep didn't bother him. With only a half a second's hesitation, he put his head down and trudged up the hill through the shrubbery, following my cues as I chose a path around the crown of the oak tree. Branches snapped underfoot and vines tore and rustled as we crashed through. In another minute we ducked under the branches of the toppled oak and were picking our way back down the steep slope to the trail.

"Whew," I said, once we were back on the path. "Glad that went okay."

"No problem," Jeri said. I could see she had a grin on her face. "We got a couple of damn good trail horses."

I smiled back. "Yep, we do." Despite the unsettling investigation we were embarked on, I found my spirits had risen and I once more felt as if I were on a pleasant walk in the woods.

We topped the ridge and rode past a water storage tank, with another big view out over the bay, and then dropped down a steep hill to a long flat trail that lay in an old roadbed. "Want to lope?" I asked Jeri.

"Sure."

I kicked Sunny up to the lope and we rocked along for a while, enjoying the breeze and the rhythmic gait. Sunlight flashed and sparkled in my eyes, shadows were like cool pools, and the tangled green forest moved by in a streaking blur. Until I saw the bridge ahead of us.

I slowed Sunny to a walk, knowing he would check himself soon. "He doesn't like this bridge," I told Jeri.

"No?"

"I don't know why exactly. He slipped on it once; maybe that's it. He's pretty good about most things, but he's liable to balk here."

The bridge was not a big one. Only three feet high, it spanned a ditch that had been washed out by erosion. There were no rails and the span was all of six feet. Not a big deal. But Sunny had been suspicious of it, and crossing it last winter he had slipped. He'd stayed up, but had approached the bridge with much caution on the return trip. I wasn't sure how he was going to feel about it now.

As I'd predicted, Sunny came to a stop in front of the obstacle and snorted. I could read his thoughts. "I want no part of this slippery little bugger."

I kicked him and clucked to him, but I could feel his resistance. He did not dance or skitter, but he took a step backward rather than forward.

I hesitated. I could "over and under" the horse with the reins and he'd go forward, but he might jump onto the bridge and perhaps slip again.

Jeri answered my unspoken question. "Why don't you just let me give you a lead. It would be safer. This horse doesn't mind bridges."

"All right," I said.

The trail was wide enough here to allow Jeri to pass me easily, and Gray Dog walked forward willingly, gave the bridge a good long look, and stepped up on it. The bridge made a hollow thunking sound under his hooves, which caused Sunny to snort again, but Gray Dog walked across it calmly and without mishaps.

I clucked to Sunny and bumped his sides with my heels. "Your turn," I said out loud.

Sunny hesitated. Once again, I knew what he was thinking. "I don't want to cross this, but the other horse did, and that's the way home." Sunny was not a stupid horse. He knew home lay across the little bridge. He snorted again, lowered his head for a better look, and then stepped cautiously forward, virtually tip-toeing onto the boards.

The bridge gave its hollow, wooden noise, but Sunny did not slip, and tip-toed safely off the other side, where Jeri was waiting.

"Why don't you lead," she said. "I don't know where I'm going."

So Sunny and I headed off down the trail again. Sunlight and shadow, tangled vines and hanging gray Spanish moss, live oaks and eucalyptus trees blended around us as we rode. We passed the high school, headed up a hill, and were once again on the ridge trail, dropping down towards the Red Barn boarding stable.

I explained to Jeri where we were. "In a minute," I said, "we'll see Ross Hart's house."

The horses picked their way carefully down the steep trail. We stepped out from behind a big manzanita bush to see the three-story A-frame below us on our left. With no less than a dozen cop cars parked around it.

Chapter 12

"WHAT THE HELL?" JERI DEMANDED as she rode up next to me.

I was too startled to say anything. I halted Sunny and gazed down at the busy scene in astonishment. There were men everywhere, some in uniform, some not, some, to my amazement, with drawn guns. The cars were green, which indicated the sheriff's department.

"Are you busting him?" I asked.

"I'm not," Jeri answered grimly. "I have no idea what this is about. But I'm going to find out. Let's go."

We trooped on down the ridge to the Red Barn and turned left, up the hill, to the house surrounded by cop cars. Quite a few spectators were gathered, including a couple, like us, mounted on horses. They'd clearly ridden up from the boarding stable to see what was going on.

Several uniformed officers were holding the spectators back from the driveway. A guy in plainclothes with a big and very obvious gun in his hand stood near them. Something about this thick-necked cop was familiar to me.

Jeri dismounted from her horse, handed me the reins, and walked up to the thick-necked cop. They looked at each other with what seemed to me to be mutual dislike, and though I couldn't hear their conversation, I had the sense it was an argument.

I rode Sunny and led Gray Dog up to a woman mounted on a paint mare. "Hi," I said. "Do you know what's going on?"

"Not exactly." The woman looked about my age and had hair that was equally blond and gray and many lines around sharp blue-gray eyes. Her mare stood in a relaxed slouch, unalarmed by all the excitement around her. The rider looked over at me and my horses and seemed to decide that as a fellow equestrian I must be all right. "That's where the trainer and barn manager live," she said quietly. "I think they're getting busted. Judging by the plants I saw those cops carrying out of the house, it's for growing pot."

"Oh," I said, thinking that Blue and I had been right about that light. "Have you seen Tammi or Ross?" I asked her.

"Nope. I heard somebody say that they took off when they saw the first cop car drive up to the house. Apparently they were down in the arena at the time."

"So they just drove away?"

"Um, I heard they rode away."

"On their horses?"

"That's what I heard."

I stared at the woman, somewhat disbelieving. Ross and Tammi had simply taken off on their horses and ridden up into the hills at the sight of cops pulling up to their house?

"Wow," I said, "if that's true, I wonder where they plan to go. It's not like they can hide out up there forever with no gear or food."

"I know." The woman half smiled. "I thought it was pretty funny, actually. Do you suppose the sheriffs will bring in a mounted posse to chase them down?"

We grinned at each other; the notion clearly amused both of us.

Jeri seemed to be done with her conversation; she came walking my way with an annoyed look on her face. Once she was back on Gray Dog and we were headed down the road and well away from the house she said, "That damn Matt Johnson."

"Is he the cop you were talking to?"

"Yep. He's head of narcotics. He and I have never gotten along.

Apparently he got a tip last week that these people were growing pot and decided on the big bust. Without informing any other department. Communication isn't always real good around the sheriff's office." I could see Jeri shake her head. "He's supposed to let everyone know in case there's a conflict. And guess what?"

"What?" I said as we rode across the vacant lot between the boarding stable and the road.

"The person who called in the tip was Jane Kelly. Last Friday."

"The day before she was shot. Oh my God." I was adding two plus two and getting the inevitable four. "She told me she'd seen Ross Hart out riding and that he'd been up to some stuff he shouldn't be up to. Then she said, 'I told him so.' And then she got shot. What if she called him on this pot growing thing and threatened to turn him in?"

"I was thinking the same thing," Jeri said grimly. "If Matt had only told me what was going on, I could have had a nice little interview with Mr. Ross Hart. But now he's disappeared."

"Along with Tammi. I was told they took off into the hills on their horses."

"Is that right?" Jeri laughed. "Matt didn't mention that part to me. I wonder how he plans to handle that?"

By this time we'd reached the road and were halted, side by side on the shoulder, waiting for a traffic-free moment to cross. When no cars were in sight, I kicked Sunny up. Jeri was right beside me as we clip-clopped over the pavement and up the narrow strip of road that led to my front gate.

"What are you going to do now?" I asked her.

"Haul this horse back to his pasture. Then I'm gonna have a couple of the guys meet me and go check out Buddy and his camper. I want to see if he's got a gun up there—I think he has, judging by the shells I found. They looked fresh. After that I want to talk to that guy with the white dog. And I'll find out if Matt and his guys have managed to pick up Ross and Tammi."

"Sounds like a busy day," I said, thanking my lucky stars that I had no further plans besides watering the garden and exercising Henry.

"Oh for a quiet life," Jeri said, as if she could read my mind. "Thanks for taking me on this ride; it really helped me get a feeling for the situation."

We'd reached my barnyard and Jeri swung off her horse briskly. "I've got to get going," she said as she slipped his bridle off and loaded him in the trailer.

"Keep me posted," I told her, and watched her drive away.

I took my time unsaddling Sunny and brushing him. It was almost two o'clock and Mac would be home soon. I filled the water troughs and watered my potted plants and in another ten minutes Blue's pickup came driving in, with Mac in the passenger seat. My son bounced out of the truck, as eager to be home as he was to arrive at the next destination.

"Want to exercise Henry?" I asked. "He needs it."

"Sure," Mac said.

"I think you can ride him bareback if you want," I said. "The vets at the equine hospital okayed that."

"Great," Mac said.

Since Henry had been operated on three months ago, we had hand-walked him daily. But now, at the three-month marker, we'd been given permission to ride him bareback at the walk. Mac was grinning from ear to ear as he caught his horse.

I was grinning, too, as I helped him slip the bridle on Henry. Henry had that effect on you. Something about his bright copper red color and cheerful white-striped face made everybody smile. I said a small silent prayer of gratitude as I legged Mac up on Henry's shiny sorrel back. Our good old horse was still with us. Still sound, too. Rehabbing Henry from major surgery had been a long road, and an expensive one, but worth the time and money. I watched Mac ride away on his steady, reliable gelding and knew I'd make the same choice again. Henry was part of the family.

Mac rode Henry for twenty minutes at the walk and then put him back in his corral. I fed the horses and headed up the hill for some much needed porch time. I could hear Blue playing his bagpipes in the little house, so I aimed for the front porch of the main house. In another five minutes I had a cup of tea and was settled in my chair. But I wasn't peaceful.

My mind was full of endless chatter. If I rested my eyes on the landmark tree the first thing I thought of was Buddy's camper. Buddy could see the landmark tree, too. From Buddy my thoughts went to Brandon Carter, hiking through the woods with his rifle in his hand. Jeri seemed sure that this was not the gun that killed Jane; still, it was an oddly ominous image. And then there were Doug and Sheryl, wrapped in what was obviously a taut dialogue—about what? And Ross Hart, busted because of Jane's tip. The noisy, restless thoughts went on and on.

I stared at the familiar ridgeline in consternation. Underlying the thoughts was something else. An edgy, uncomfortable feeling. It didn't take me long to figure it out. I was afraid. I pictured myself riding the trails alone, seeing Brandon, perhaps Buddy—without Jeri at my side. And fear twisted in my gut.

I didn't like it. I had ridden the trails along the ridge for so long, in all seasons and weather; they were part of my life, part of my home. I took a sip of my steaming tea and felt anger rise up underneath the fear. As on the day Jane had been murdered, after the racing thoughts and the fear came resistance. This was my home. Those were our trails. I didn't want all of it polluted by an ugly dangerous blight. I didn't want to be afraid to go there. But what exactly could I do about it?

The answer that came to me was simple and startling.

Then go there.

I took another sip of tea and wondered what that meant.

Just go there.

That was it. No explanation. But I thought I understood. If I didn't want the woods to be forever haunted, I could not run. I had to stay and fight.

Tomorrow, I promised myself, I'll go for a ride on the ridge. Alone.

Chapter 13

I SADDLED SUNNY AROUND ten o'clock the next morning, determined to go for a ride. Blue had taken Mac to his karate class; I thought I had a couple of free hours in which no one would miss me. And I planned to spend them on the trails.

I wasn't sure if this was a wise course of action. In fact, I was damned nervous about it. But the very anxiety that tensed my jaw and clenched my stomach made me more stubborn. I wasn't going to be run off my home range. In my cargo pockets I had a cell phone and a camera. I'd debated bringing my pistol, but rejected the idea as unworkable. I couldn't see myself in some sort of western shootout. Besides, the only place I could carry the gun was in a saddlebag, and how was I supposed to get it out in time to be effective if someone actually shot at me? Let alone, how was Sunny going to feel about having a gun fired off his back?

It ain't gonna happen, I reassured myself as I pulled the cinch tight and climbed on. You're just going for a ride on the familiar trails. You probably won't see a soul.

I didn't plan to go anywhere near Buddy's camper, that was for sure. But even riding Sunny down my own driveway, I felt unnaturally alert, as if I had eyes in the back of my head—eyes that were scanning for something hiding in the brush. Something or someone. The vision of some unknown person concealed in the shrubbery with a loaded gun pointed my way just wouldn't leave me.

We crossed the road without incident—for once there was very little traffic. Planning my route in my mind, I chose the little side-hill trail that skirted the big subdivision. I hadn't taken Jeri that way, partly because I wasn't keen to reveal the existence of this trail. But it was the way I most often went myself.

I rode across the meadow where we had seen the coyote on Sunday, and headed up the hill through the oak trees. The sudden shift from brilliant light to deep shadow felt like stepping into a cave. But in a minute my eyes adjusted and the filtered light under the oaks was pleasantly dim.

Moving through the trees on my steady yellow horse felt familiar and reassuring, and slowly the tight fear in my gut began to soften and melt. The woods did not seem ominous, as I had dreaded; they were their same old selves, green and friendly. As we topped the first hill, I peered through the screen of tree branches at the big houses along Storybook Road.

Blank, well-tended, silent, the houses struck me as ominous. Repulsive, and yes, ominous. I shook my head at the thought. Did I suppose the shooter was crouched in one of these ugly modern mansions? Not likely. But the persistent image of the friendly woods and hostile houses stuck in my mind.

We made our way along the ridge, winding between twisted tree trunks, tangled scrub, and twining vines. I ducked for the low overhanging branch. Sunny clambered up the hills and stepped carefully down into the gullies. Every now and then I glanced down through the leaves to see glimpses of the tidy lawns and patios that skirted the giant, featureless houses on the other side of the ridge. I was hidden behind a screen of manzanita and scrub oak, invisible to any but a discerning eye, yet I still felt vulnerable. As if some adversary might spot me.

In another minute or two we topped the ridge and made our way down the slope, through the warm meadow, headed toward the spot where I'd found Jane's body. The crime scene tape was still there, but no one was around. I heaved a sigh of relief. Maybe this was going to be just another pleasant walk in the woods. I averted my eyes from the spot where Jane's corpse had rested.

Sunny paced along; the air was warm and fresh. I took a deep breath. I was past the crime tape and my mind felt clear. I looked down to see brilliant white and gold light sparks reflected on the left side of Sunny's shiny neck. His mane sprang in a snowy crest to sweep down the other side. In front of me his yellow ears were pricked sharply forward, almost touching at the tips. And suddenly I was happy.

I rode down the warm meadow and into the cold valley. Across the streambed and up through the redwood grove. I let Sunny trot up the hill, which he clearly wished to do. Then back down to the walk through tangles of wild currant and berry vines. Up ahead was the three-way trail crossing. And then I heard voices.

Immediately my cheerful mood vanished and my heart thumped hard in my chest. There was no rational reason. Someone who meant to shoot at me would probably not be chatting out loud. But I couldn't help it. My nerves were strung as tight as a spooky horse.

I peered ahead and checked Sunny, not sure I wanted to meet anyone out here in the woods. I could hear the voices but I couldn't make out what they were saying. They were not loud; the tone sounded conversational, not confrontational.

Sunny and I stood in a clump of greenery where the trail detoured around a toppled oak. The voices appeared to be coming from the clearing where the three trails met, right at the top of the slope, perhaps a hundred feet away. Male voices, it sounded like. Just chatting.

I hesitated and then bumped Sunny with my heels. What danger could there be? Sunny walked calmly forward and up the hill; in another minute I could see the figures standing in the clearing, both on foot. They looked familiar, and in a moment I recognized them. The hiker with his yellow Lab, and Brandon, carrying his rifle. As before, the hiker carried a machete. Almost without thinking, I halted Sunny.

It was just too creepy—two men with weapons up in the woods. They had spotted me, and both men were looking in my direction.

"Um, hello," I said, from fifty feet away.

Brandon nodded his head in response; the hiker muttered something inaudible to me. And both turned and moved off, in different directions.

The man and dog headed down the ridge trail; Brandon came towards me. My eyes were fixed on the rifle, which he held loosely in one hand, not pointing it at anything. It still made me nervous. I reined Sunny off to the side of the trail as Brandon approached.

"Nice day for a hike," I said.

Brandon ignored this, except to jerk his chin in response, as before. As he came up to us, I tried again. "Didn't I meet you yesterday?"

At this he stopped and looked up, meeting my eyes. His were startlingly blue, the bluest eyes I'd ever seen. "You were with the sheriff lady," he said.

"Yep," I agreed.

"Seen any cougars lately?"

"Nope," I said.

Laconic as Brandon had sounded, I did not get the sense he was unfriendly. Just reserved. His blue eyes looked up at me in a steady, curious way. He held the rifle pointed loosely at the ground. For a second I hesitated.

"Are you looking for the shooter?" It just popped out of my mouth.

Brandon studied me a minute. "Maybe," he said at last.

For some reason, I found this reassuring. It struck me that Brandon was being honest.

"Why?" I asked.

"I don't like people shooting women up in the woods."

I had the feeling that Brandon's emotions were similar to mine. A deep-down anger at the evil that had polluted our ridge.

"I don't like it either," I said. "I don't want to be afraid to come here."

"I hear you," he said.

"What did the guy with the dog have to say?" I asked.

"Nothing much. He walks up here with the dog every day. He said he hasn't seen anything unusual. Have you?"

"No," I said. "Not today. Did you see that camper up on the logging road?"

"It's gone now," Brandon said.

"It is?"

"That dude took off yesterday. I saw the camper driving down the road."

"Oh," I said, and wondered if Jeri had managed to get back to Buddy before he departed.

Brandon was still looking up at me, but I couldn't think of anything else to add to this conversation. Still, somehow I felt sure that he and I were on the same side. After a moment he ducked his head, said, "Have a nice ride," and walked on past. I watched him go, feeling confused and puzzled. There was something odd about this guy. And yet I kind of liked him.

I bumped Sunny with my heels and sent him forward. The hiker and his dog had disappeared. I rode up to the three-way trail crossing, and took the trail that led to the Lookout. With any luck I was done encountering folks for the day.

Sunny walked briskly through a tunnel of scrub oaks and vines that arched overhead and marched quickly up the steep hill beyond. He knew which way we were going, and that he would be allowed to have a rest at the Lookout. Best for him to get it over with and get there. Sunny broke into a trot and we moved steadily uphill between redwoods and then some old, tall madrones. I slowed the horse to the walk as the ground leveled out. We passed the poacher's blind high in the oak tree and I glanced up automatically. Nothing to be seen. A moment later later we arrived in the little clearing at the top of the bluff, Sunny huffing slightly but composed. Only to find another horseman planted in front of the view.

It took me all of a second to recognize Jonah Wakefield on his buckskin colt. Jonah was wearing his Stetson and long duster and leading a saddled sorrel horse by the bridle reins. He did not seem aware that I was there.

Jonah might not have been aware of me and Sunny, but both of his horses spotted us quickly. Ears went up, heads raised; the buckskin nickered. Jonah looked over his shoulder and saw me.

"Hello," he said.

"Hi," I returned. I was studying the horse he led, which looked familiar. "Is that Sheryl Silverman's mare?" I asked.

"Yeah, it is," he said. "Have you seen her?"

"Me?" I was surprised by his question. "No, I haven't seen her. Why?"

"I found this mare grazing in the field outside our back gate. She was dragging her bridle reins and from the look of them she'd been there awhile. I'm afraid she might have dumped Sheryl out here somewhere. So I went looking for her."

I shook my head. "I haven't seen her. I haven't seen any horse people this morning. Just a couple of hikers."

"I guess I'll ride back down the logging road and the swingset trail. That's the way she usually went, I think." Jonah tugged on the sorrel mare and rode off, looking worried.

I sighed. Somehow contemplating the view didn't seem as appealing now. I glanced over my shoulder; I had no wish to ride the same way as Jonah. And then I remembered it. The new trail.

Mac had spotted it on Google Earth one day. The faint mark of a trail leading from the Lookout back towards our place—a trail we'd never ridden.

I walked Sunny across the clearing and sure enough, there it was. A faint, dusty track leading off down the hill, well marked with horse hoofprints. In the sunlight it appeared entirely benign, a gentle slope of dried grass the only apparent terrain.

Still, I hesitated. I knew where this trail ended up, more or less—it went the right way to take me home. But I didn't know what it traversed exactly. Would I end up in some steep, tricky spot where I didn't at all want to be? I had no wish to hurt my horse or myself. And I had done enough trail riding to be wary of unknown trails.

Still, other horses went this way—that was plain. If they could do it, surely we could do it, too. Mentally I rebutted this easily. Other horses could be ridden by wild teenagers who had no idea of danger, or savvy endurance riders mounted on handy Arabs that could handle any amount of adversity. I, on the other hand, was a relatively sedate middle-aged woman on an equally sedate middle-aged horse. Neither one of us wanted to pick our way down a cliff.

Somehow, though, I found myself letting Sunny take the new trail. The allure of seeing something different was overwhelming my natural caution. I'll turn back, I told myself, if it gets tricky.

We walked down the dusty hillside and into a pretty grove of redwood trees. The trail wound between their giant trunks, presenting no problems, easy to follow, obviously well traveled. I began to relax.

Down and down we went, traversing the opposite side of the ridge from the one we'd come up. Here we ducked under the overhanging branches of an oak tree, there we detoured around a clump of brambles. The trail was plain. And then it came to a steep dropoff.

Horses went down here. The tracks were well marked in the soft ground, dug deep by many scrambling hooves. I reined Sunny to a stop. Did I really want to go down this? It looked as though we might have to slide all the way to the bottom, and that was quite a ways—maybe fifty feet.

On the other hand, did I really want to retrace my steps and go back? Not so much. If I could just get down this bit, maybe the rest would be easy. Sunny was the master of a cautious descent. I clucked to him and felt him step forward.

Slowly, very slowly, Sunny shuffled his way down the hill, one careful baby step at a time. Occasionally his back feet slid a bit, but he remained calm, stayed up, and kept shuffling down the steep chute. I didn't hurry him, just tried to sit balanced and quiet on his nearly vertical-seeming back as he made his way down the bank.

Once at the bottom I heaved a sigh of relief. The sun spangled the trail, blue jays squawked in the trees. For the past minute, I had not thought once about the shooter in the woods. I almost laughed. Nothing like a little real and present danger to drive away the "what ifs."

The trail continued on through the forest. Sunny walked out, ears forward, looking around. I thought I knew about where we were—but I wasn't sure. Somewhere on the west side of the ridge. Somewhere I'd never been before.

The trail made a bend and started steadily upward. I looked ahead and checked Sunny abruptly. Now this I did not like. Not fifty feet ahead of me the route became very steep indeed, and in the middle of the most vertical bit, the path made a sharp right-angle turn to dodge a huge redwood stump, and in the midst of the turn was a two foot step up over the root. A slip and a scramble here could have dire results.

Well, damn. I could see daylight shining through the trees above—it looked as though I would be out of the forest if I could get past the steep part. I was dying to know exactly where this trail was taking me. And turning back now would involve going up the equally steep place with the deep ground that Sunny had slithered down. I was not anxious to try scrambling up through the loose dirt. But I was not keen on what I saw ahead either.

Sunny relaxed and cocked a hind leg as I stared at the trail, wondering what I ought to do. My steady mount was willing to sit here all day, while I pondered, for which I was profoundly grateful.

Thick tangles of blackberry vines banked either side of the trail, but after a minute I noticed that the vegetation was trampled and beaten down to my left. I studied this for a moment. It looked as though some horses had gone this way. In another moment I was sure that other horsemen had elected an alternate route up the hill, which avoided the right-angle turn and the step up. There wasn't much of a trail, just the battered streak through the foliage, but I was instantly sure that was the way to go.

"Come on, Sunny." I clucked, and reined my little yellow horse to the left. He obediently plowed through the brambles and we followed the route up and over the crest with no trouble. In a minute we emerged through the shrubbery onto an old roadbed. Aha. Now I knew where we were.

I reined Sunny to the right. "This is that old road that runs behind the high school," I said out loud. "It'll take us right where we need to go."

Somehow the sound of my voice did not seem cheering, as I had imagined it would. I felt quite cheerful, having solved my current dilemma, but the words echoed oddly in the empty woods. I glanced over my shoulder, suddenly reminded of the shooter. Nothing to be seen, just sunlight laying a golden swath across the yellow dried grass of autumn, which choked the roadbed. Tangles of poison oak, coyote brush, and blackberry brambles fringed the verges.

I followed the roadbed along the base of the ridge, headed in the direction of home. Ahead of me a row of ancient cypress trees marked some old human doings. The trees would not have grown in a row like this naturally. The cypress had a dark and somber look.

I had never been this way before, though I had noticed the roadbed in the past and wondered where it went. It suddenly struck me that the bowl-like depression ahead of me, skirted by the row of cypress on one side, was an old reservoir. It lay at the base of the ridge, and when riding the ridge trail in the spring, I always heard frogs peeping down here and had wondered where the water was. Voilà. Now I knew.

This pleased me in a small way; I remained constantly interested in the little details of the ridge and its flora, fauna, and topography. Sunny paced quietly through the late morning sunshine into the shadows of the cypress trees, following the road which led past the base of the trees and along what was once the dike of a reservoir. I peered down at a small pond of dark water at the bottom of the deep hollow. Still some water there, even in October. It must have been an important water source, long ago. There seemed to be a little trail leading down to the pool. I looked harder. Someone was there. Someone in jeans and a denim jacket, apparently taking a nap down near the water.

The person lay face down in a patch of dried grass. My first thought was that it was one of the many street people who ranged Santa Cruz County. I halted Sunny and stared. There was something odd about this. My impulse was to ride on by and stay out of trouble, but I stifled it. I started Sunny down the faint trail that led to the pond.

Sunny walked very slowly; he would have preferred to keep on in the direction of home. After we had gone halfway down the trail I halted him again. The figure hadn't moved. But surely it was female, with a long blond braid.

And a dozen thoughts went crashing through my mind. Sheryl. Sheryl's horse found riderless, wearing a saddle; the shooter. Oh my God. This was Sheryl; I was sure of it.

"Sheryl!" I shouted, hoping against hope that she was just taking a nap.

The figure did not move, and I kicked Sunny forward. We half walked, half trotted down the slope to the pool, and I heaved myself off the horse and wrapped his reins around a branch.

"Sheryl!" I said again as I approached her.

No doubt in my mind that this was Sheryl. The form, the clothes, the long blond braid. Even as I reached her and put a hand on the denim of her jacket, a part of my mind noted that the fabric was damp and cold. I shook her gently and my hand jerked back in shock. The body was stiff. She had been dead awhile.

Gritting my teeth, I forced myself to wrestle the cold, stiff form over enough to see the face, to be sure. It was Sheryl, all right. I shivered and lowered her back into her original position. My head swam and I sat down on the ground. No need to check to be sure if she was dead. I still could not see what had caused her demise, but I wasn't game to look. This dark little hollow, with its pool of black, brackish water, struck me as ominous and full of shadows that I did not like. I could not help Sheryl. I was getting out of here.

Shoving myself to my feet, I ignored my whirling brain and stepped quickly up to Sunny, untied him, and climbed back on. I did not care if my cell phone would work from here or not. I was going home first. Then I'd call. No damn way was I waiting here in this spot beside that body for help, I didn't care what protocol demanded. I could not help Sheryl and I wanted out of this place.

Kicking Sunny up to the trot, I zipped up the little trail and onto the roadbed. Here I let him take the lope. We checked briefly to clamber over a few downed tree trunks and then loped the rest of the way through the lower skirts of the Five Thousand Eucalyptus Forest, until we reached the trail that led past the house of the white dog. The dog did not appear today and I loped through the acacia trees and on over the hill to the back lot of Red Barn Stable. I didn't spare a glance to see who was or wasn't visible there. I was going home.

I slowed Sunny to the walk as we approached the road, and tried to focus through my seething thoughts. My God. Sheryl was dead. I could not escape the dread that she had been shot, just like Jane. What in the hell was happening here?

The traffic cleared and we crossed; I let Sunny trot up the last hill and through my gate. A quick glance told me that Blue and Mac weren't back yet; I gave thanks for that. I took the time to unsaddle Sunny and turn him back out in his corral before I went up to the house and picked up the phone. Taking a deep breath, I dialed Jeri Ward's cell.

Chapter 14

JERI ANSWERED ON THE SECOND RING, sounding some-what frazzled—for Jeri. "Ward here."

"Jeri, it's Gail. I found another body in the woods. It's Sheryl Silverman."

"What? Where? Are you there now?" Intensity fairly crackled in Jeri's voice.

"No, I'm home."

"What? Are you sure she's dead? Where is she?"

"She's dead. I'm pretty sure she's been dead all night." I swallowed. "I can show you where she is. You know the guy with the white dog that chased us yesterday? Meet me at the end of his driveway."

"I'll be there in five minutes."

I hung up the phone and walked out to my truck. Blue and Mac were still not back. Good. That made things easier. I got in the truck and headed off down the drive. It didn't take me five minutes to reach the driveway of the white dog, but Jeri was there before me.

I parked my truck and climbed into her car. Neither of us wasted any words.

"Drive up here, until you get to the place where the trail crosses the driveway," I told her.

"Okay. How far do we have to walk after that?"

"Not far. About a quarter mile. The body is down by an old reservoir."

"How did you happen to find it?"

"Riding in the woods. I took a new trail. Well, new to me. I'd never been that way before. Never seen this pond in my life. But that's where I found her."

"Shot?" Jeri's tone was terse.

"I don't know. She was face down, stiff and cold. I think she'd been there all night. I only moved her enough to be sure about that. I didn't roll her over. I don't know what killed her. It wasn't obvious."

By this time we'd reached the trail, and Jeri parked the sheriff's sedan on the side of the driveway. "Hope this makes him worry," she snapped as we climbed out of the car, looking over her shoulder at the light blue house that was clearly visible at the end of the drive.

"Who? The white dog guy?"

"Yeah, him. Bill Waters." Jeri was behind me as I led off along the trail, headed uphill. I could hear her voice clearly. "I went to talk to him yesterday. He was pretty belligerent. Full of crap about how the horses had no right to be coming through here. The trail is actually on the neighbor's property, and that neighbor is fine with it, but this guy is just really hostile. I'm not sure why."

"Well," I said, huffing a little as I marched steadily uphill as quickly as I could. "That house is the closest dwelling to where this body is located. And I'm willing to bet she was riding a horse when she arrived at the pond. Maybe you should call on the guy again, seeing as how he's so hostile to horse people. See if he has a twenty-two pistol or rifle."

"Why are you sure she was horseback?"

"She was a rider, not a hiker, as far as I know. And I saw Jonah Wakefield this morning. He told me he'd found her mare grazing outside the back gate. He was leading the mare around, said he was looking for Sheryl."

"Did you see anyone else?"

"Yeah. Brandon Carter and the hiker with the yellow Lab. Brandon says that guy hikes up here a lot."

"Brandon, huh?" Jeri sounded out of breath, too.

We half jogged on up the hill, keeping a brisk pace. Both of us were quiet now, conserving our breath for hiking. We were in the skirts of the eucalyptus forest. I turned right off the trail onto the old roadbed. Ahead of me I could see the dark tops of the cypress trees that lined the lower edge of the reservoir.

"It's there," I said, pointing the trees out to Jeri.

She nodded; we both kept marching on. It was almost noon and sunlight dappled the ground around us; the air was warm. I was starting to sweat. Still, I shivered as we reached the row of cypress. The depression that held the pond was on our left. I clambered over a couple of downed tree trunks, almost trotting, and reached the faint path that led down to the brackish pool of water. The denim-clad figure was there, lying as I had left her. I halted.

Jeri moved past me instantly, scrambling quickly down the hill, ignoring the brambles and poison oak that choked the trail. I stayed where I was. I wanted no more close-up views of dead bodies.

Jeri reached the corpse and surveyed it carefully. She touched the hand for a second and then, very carefully, and with some effort, rolled the body halfway over and peered at it. Then she lowered it again. For a second she stayed frozen, her eyes sweeping the area, and then she headed back up the hill to me.

"Did you ride your horse down here?" she asked me.

"Yes. I tied him to that tree." And I pointed. "I looked at the body very much as you did, but I didn't roll her over that far. Was she shot?" I asked.

"Just like the other one," Jeri said tersely. "We've got a problem. I'm calling the crime-scene guys now." She was digging her cell phone out of her pocket as she spoke.

"I need to go home," I said, turning around. "You can find me later, all right?"

Jeri nodded; I was already moving swiftly up the trail. I had no wish to meet up with the crime-scene guys. I wanted to go home.

Fifteen minutes later I was there, unimpeded. I shut my front gate behind me, hoping against hope that it might keep trouble from my door. But I knew better. Jeri would be back, wanting my statement. And there was no way around it, we already had trouble, here in my little part of the hills. These two shootings were almost certainly connected. One woman shot out riding might have been an accident. Two women, shot in exactly the same way, riding in the same area, could not possibly be by chance. Someone had wanted them dead.

I shivered as I drove up the hill. Blue's truck was parked in its familiar place; I wondered how exactly to explain this new development to Mac. As it turned out, I didn't have to.

Mac and Blue were out in the yard, playing with a very small black dog that I had never seen before. Mac turned a joyful face to me as I climbed out of my pickup.

"Look, Mama, we got a new dog!"

"So I see," I said, staring at the leaping little creature. "Um, what is it?"

"We don't know," Mac said proudly. "Someone was giving them away at the grocery store. They said she's part Chihuahua, part terrier, part who knows."

The little dog was certainly cute. I bent down and called her and she ran to me eagerly, wagging her tail. She was black, with coarse, wiry terrier hair and whiskers, like Freckles. She was obviously going to be bigger than a Chihuahua, maybe twenty pounds at most, though. A little black, whiskery mutt.

"See the white star on her chest?" Mac said. "We named her Star."

Blue was grinning.

"And you okayed this?" I asked him.

"Well, you have been saying you want to get another dog. And Freckles is pretty old."

"That's true," I agreed.

"And you said you wanted a small dog."

"Well, yeah, I guess I did."

"She's little, Mama," Mac said, playing tug-of-war with Star. "Do you like her?"

I smiled. "Yes, I like her. Does Freckles like her?"

I glanced at the old dog, who was basking in the sun, apparently indifferent to the newcomer.

"She seems okay with it," Blue said. "She just growls if the puppy jumps on her. Otherwise she wags her tail. She won't play with her, though."

"I guess she's too old for that," I said. "As long as she doesn't eat her."

"She's not showing any sign of it. And look..." And Blue gestured at Mac, who was running laps around the riding ring with the puppy hot on his heels.

"Yeah," I said. "He was ready for a puppy. Well, good, I guess. But Blue..." And in another minute I had told him about finding Sheryl's body and Jeri's immenint arrival.

Blue's smile faded as I spoke and his face looked stern. "Gail, I think it's time we stopped riding and hiking in the woods for a while. Until this is resolved, anyway."

"I know," I said. "I agree with you. I just hope it gets resolved soon. Let's not mention it to Mac, okay? I don't want him to be afraid of the woods. We just won't go up there as a family until this is over."

"If it's ever over," Blue said glumly. "Not all crimes get solved."

I stared at him and shook my head. Mac was running through the sunshine with his puppy, the ridge a peaceful, dark green background behind him. The thought of an unknown and frightening evil lurking there forever almost made my stomach turn.

"It WILL get solved," I said, a little too fiercely. "It has to."

Blue glanced at me oddly, but Mac and the prancing puppy were upon us, and we both dropped the subject and began to play with the little dog.

In another hour Star was sacked out on the couch along with

Freckles, lunch had been eaten, and Jeri's car was coming up the driveway. By this time her visits had become routine and neither Blue nor Mac paid much attention as I excused myself and went over to the other house to meet her.

Jeri was seated on the couch and fiddling with her recorder when I walked in. I took a deep breath, striving for a patient, tranquil mind, and sat down in the rocking chair.

"What did you learn?" I asked her.

"Unofficially, it looks as though she was shot with a twenty-two in the chest, just like the other woman. It does appear that she was probably horseback; we saw fresh hoofprints very near where she lay and you didn't ride there, right?"

"No, I never rode Sunny within fifty feet of her body."

"That's what I thought." Jeri clicked her recorder on. "Okay, tell the story of how you found her."

I recounted the morning's expedition as it had happened, leaving out no detail I could remember. When I was done Jeri clicked the recorder off and sat silently, a moody expression on her face.

"Did you get a chance to talk to Buddy?" I asked.

"Buddy's camper was gone when I got up there yesterday afternoon about four o'clock," Jeri said. "I guess our friend Brandon saw him drive out. I'll have to talk to Brandon. The question is, was Sheryl Silverman shot before that? Or that's one question, anyway."

Jeri was quiet a moment. "I went back to Lazy Valley yesterday afternoon after I put Gray Dog back in his pasture. I saw Doug Martin and talked to him. Didn't learn much. He said Sheryl had gone out for a ride. Judging by the condition of that body, I'm guessing she was shot that afternoon. So why didn't Doug report her as missing?"

"Good question," I said. But even as the words left my mouth I was picturing Doug's handsome, boyish face and feeling sure he was no killer. Then I remembered the strangely intense expressions on his and Sheryl's faces and their odd body language when

I had last seen them, as Jeri and I had ridden through Lazy Valley. Maybe it was better not to assume anything.

Jeri stood up. "I need to get over to Lazy Valley and find Doug Martin," she said. "If he's not there I'll have a look at Jane Kelly's place." She was headed for the door when she stopped and looked over her shoulder at me. "We still haven't managed to pick up Ross Hart and Tammi Martinez," she said. "They haven't gone back to their house or to the Red Barn, that we know of. They just disappeared."

"Wow," I said. "That's weird. Do you think they're hiding out up on the ridge? They took off with just the clothes on their backs as I heard it. I can't believe they'll last very long camping out up there. I wonder who's feeding the horses at the Red Barn?"

Jeri shrugged. "No idea. Got to go."

And she was gone.

I got up out of my rocker and went out on the porch. Jeri's car was bumping down the driveway. I could see the three horses in their corrals, tails swishing lazily. Chickadees pecked at the seeds in the drooping sunflowers that towered over the vegetable garden fence. A skim of clouds drifted like a wraith across the sun and a chilly little breeze brushed my cheek. It felt like the weather might be changing.

I was restless as that wind. Too much was happening, too much was unknown. I wanted to do something, but didn't know what it should be. For a second, thoughts chased through my mind... Doug Martin's face, Sheryl's cold body, Buddy and his camper, and the disappearance of Ross and Tammi. And suddenly I made up my mind. I was going to visit the Red Barn. Find out if they needed any help feeding. It was the least I could do.

Chapter 15

TEN MINUTES LATER I'D TOLD Blue and Mac where I was going and was walking down my driveway. Mac was playing fetch with Star and Blue was napping. I'd donned a denim jacket to combat the wind, which was steadily increasing. Storm coming, it felt like.

It was roughly four o'clock when I strolled in the drive that led to the Red Barn. There were several people in the arena and lots more hanging around the barn and shedrow. Everyone seemed to be very busy talking. I looked about for someone I recognized.

In a minute I spotted the woman with the blond/gray hair mucking out the paint mare's pen. I drifted over in her direction and leaned on the rails of the pen. The woman stopped her shoveling and glanced at me curiously.

"Hi. I'm Gail McCarthy," I said. "I'm a neighbor. I talked to you yesterday after the big bust. Has anybody heard what happened to Ross and Tammi?"

The woman pushed a strand of hair out of her eyes and squinted at me. "I'm Riva," she said. "And no, no one here seems to know where Ross and Tammi went or what their plans are."

"Do you think they're hiding up in the woods?" I asked idly.

"Seems unlikely to me," Riva said. "Not those two. They liked their comforts."

"That was my impression, too," I said. "Who's doing the feeding?"

"We're all feeding our own," Riva answered. "Thus the crowd." And she gestured around. "A few people are starting to develop little cooperative groups, now that we all realize they might not be coming back. Apparently they didn't want to be busted. Someone called the barn owner, who moved to town after she brought Tammi in to manage the place. Hopefully she'll come up with a new manager."

"Did Tammi do all the feeding?"

"Along with Ross. And we all clean our own stalls and pens. They didn't have any regular barn help."

"Oh," I said. The Red Barn had always been known as a "cheap" boarding stable.

Riva had returned to shoveling poop and I watched her awhile. "Do you ride the trails much?" I asked at last.

Riva paused and looked at me. "I used to," she said. "I haven't felt much like getting out there since Jane was killed."

"I understand," I said. "I guess we're all wondering how that happened," I added, deciding not to mention Sheryl.

Riva kept meeting my eyes. "Do you know who Bill is?" she asked.

"Um, no, I don't think so." I was puzzled by the intensity in her voice.

"Bill lives in a blue house near the trail in that direction." Riva waved a hand. "And he owns a big white dog."

"Oh, that guy," I said. "Yeah, I do know who you mean. He sics his dog on horse people."

"And he's trying to block the trails," Riva added fiercely.

"He's the one who's doing that?" I asked. "I've seen those roadblocks. How do you know it was him?"

"I saw him doing it one day. Blocking the ridge trail. Sat there on my horse and watched him for a while. Then I said, 'What the hell do you think you're doing? This isn't your land.' And he gave me what I can only describe as an evil look. You know what he said? 'I don't like horses on that trail looking down at my house. We don't need any horse people around here. And if you're smart, you'll stay off these trails.'"

"He said that? Wow."

"It was creepy. I had the thought then and there that if that guy has a gun he'd be dangerous. I turned around and rode away from him right away. The next thing I hear, Jane has gone and called the sheriffs on him for siccing the white dog on people. And the next thing Jane gets shot. What would you think?"

"I see what you mean," I said. And the thought leaped into my mind. Someone shooting horse people not because they were simply nuts, as I had thought Buddy might be, but because they were irrationally anti-horse. And Sheryl had been shot very near this guy's house. Damn. This was information I should share with Jeri.

I shivered, as a gust of chilly wind blew through the yard, and drew my denim jacket more closely around me. Riva had gone back to raking and shoveling. "Thanks," I told her bent head. "I guess I'll get going."

"See you," she said, and picked up the loaded wheelbarrow to heave it along.

I walked down the aisle by the shedrow, headed in the direction of the road out. As I reached the gate I looked up the road to see a black horse coming down it. The coppery gold sheen of the rider's hair was distinctive. I let myself out the gate and walked up the hill toward Trish O'Hara, who was riding down from the direction of the ridge trail.

"Hey, Gail," Trish said in her friendly way as she saw me. "What's going on?"

"Lots," I said, not sure how to answer this question. "What are you up to?"

"Well, looking for Sheryl Silverman, partly. Jonah said he found her saddled horse outside the gate, but nobody's seen her. Everyone is worried that she got dumped and is hurt. So I went out for a ride, hoping I'd find her. But I haven't."

I shook my head. "Jeez, Trish. I guess I ought to tell you. I found Sheryl this morning when I was out riding."

"Is she okay?"

"No. She's dead."

"Oh no." Trish's well-meaning face reflected the shock she was undoubtedly feeling. I didn't see any reason to keep her in the dark.

"She'd been shot," I said. "Just like Jane."

"Oh no," Trish said again. "That's terrible. I should get back to Lazy Valley and tell them."

"They'll know by now," I said. "That detective I was riding with yesterday, Jeri Ward, has gone over there to ask questions. Everyone is going to know pretty soon."

"Oh my God." Trish was obviously trying to process this news. "I can't believe it. What is happening here? Is there some crazy person out there shooting horse people?"

"I don't know," I said, "but the thought crossed my mind. Have you run into that guy who lives in the house near the trail over there," I pointed, "and has a white dog?"

"Oh, the dog that chases horses." Trish shrugged. "I don't know anything about the owner."

I recounted the story Riva had told me and said, "So now I'm wondering." Another thought struck me. "You were out riding yesterday, weren't you? Did you ride long?"

"About three hours, I guess," Trish said, sounding puzzled.

"Did you see anyone?"

"Well, you guys. And right as I was headed back I saw Ross Hart and Tammi Martinez, riding up the swingset trail at the high lope. I got out of their way and they barreled on by me, didn't even stop. It was weird."

Bingo, I thought. "Up the swingset trail, huh? Where did you see them?"

"Right where the swingset trail takes off from the logging road. I was headed up the logging road."

"Did you see the camper?"

"Yeah, there was a camper parked by the side of the road. An old beat-up one."

"Did you see the guy?"

"Nope. No guy was around the camper. Not that I saw."

"Do you know about what time this would be?"

Trish gave me an odd look, but glanced at her wrist and said, "I got back from my ride around two. I checked my watch. So I suppose I saw Ross and Tammi and the camper sometime between one and two."

That made sense. Jeri and I had arrived at the scene of the bust around one, I thought. And Tammi and Ross had ridden away shortly before then. The question was, where were they going? From the swingset trail they could take the trail that led to Tucker Pond and on to the old orchard. From there they could ride to White Road. And from there on to Harkins Valley. They could also ride down to Moon Valley and to Lazy Valley Stable. From there they could reach Highway 1. If they had their cell phones with them, it would be a simple matter to call a friend with a horse trailer to come pick them up at any of these main roads. Tammi and Ross might right now be hidden out at any number of horse places in the county. If they did not return to their home or the Red Barn, it could prove very difficult for the sheriffs to find them. Tammi and Ross could just possibly have managed a very effective disappearance.

Trish was watching my face. "So what were Ross and Tammi up to, galloping through the woods? I can tell you know something."

I told her the story of the bust and the horseback getaway, and Trish laughed. "I don't blame them," she said. "Busting people for growing pot is ridiculous. Let those stupid sheriffs work on who's killing people on the trails."

"I agree," I said. "But it also makes me wonder. Running away like that is a pretty extreme reaction. And Jane Kelly called in the tip that got Ross and Tammi busted."

"Oh," Trish said. "I see what you mean. Where did you find Sheryl?"

"Down by that old reservoir."

"Oh yeah," Trish said. "I know where that is. Poor Sheryl. I may not have liked her but I didn't wish her any harm."

"Did you see anyone when you were out riding today?"

"Not really. I saw that street guy's camp, but he wasn't around."

"What guy is that?"

"He's got long blond hair and keeps a chicken for a pet. He lives in a tent that's just near the spot where the long flat trail heads up the hill to the water tank. It's pretty well hidden from the trail."

"I've never seen that guy or his camp," I said, "but I know the spot you mean."

I reflected that those of us who rode and hiked these trails knew them pretty well. A little thought flickered through my mind and then disappeared again as a blast of wind whistled around me.

"This guy's been living there awhile," Trish said. "I think he's harmless. He hitchhikes into town and makes spare change playing his flute."

"Sounds harmless," I agreed.

Trish shook her head. "I guess we can't assume anything anymore."

For a second we were both silent. A draft of cold air swirled the fallen leaves around us and I shivered.

"Brrr," I said. "I think I'm going home. It looks like it's going to storm."

Trish glanced at the sky. "Right," she said, "Me, too. Gail, I'm going up the ridge trail straight to the Lookout and dropping down to Moon Valley from there. It should take me an hour. Can you do me a big favor?"

"Sure," I said.

"Call me on my cell phone in an hour and make sure I made it back to Lazy Valley." Reaching into her pocket, she handed me her card. "It's on there," she said.

"Will do," I said. "And I know all the trails you're talking about, so if I can't reach you I'll come after you."

"Thanks," Trish said, and reined Coal off up the hill.

I watched her receding figure for a moment—a lone red-headed woman on a black horse, with the wind whipping at dark mane and tail and bright coppery hair. Behind them the ridge loomed, stormy gusts tossing the eucalyptus trees. Trish looked solitary and forlorn, and I didn't envy her. Alone on the trails was not an appealing prospect in this moment.

Gathering the folds of my jacket around me, I hurried towards the main road and home. I needed to call Jeri Ward.

Chapter 16

I REACHED HOME TO FIND Mac wrestling with his new puppy in the hall and Blue making stew for dinner. My attempt to call Jeri reached only her answering machine. I accepted a margarita from Blue and settled into the armchair by the fire. For the first time I let myself feel how tired I was, both emotionally and physically. The horses and other critters were fed, the wind was swirling through the trees and around the house. Inside, the rich, aromatic smell of the stew and the crackle of the fire in the woodstove spoke strongly of comfort. This was a night for an early dinner and bedtime—at least for me.

But I had one more chore to do. I glanced at the clock and then dialed Trish's cell phone number. She answered on the first ring, sounding out of breath. "Hi Gail. I just got Coal put away. You won't believe what's going on around here."

"What?" I said.

"Apparently that detective showed up out here at Lazy Valley while Doug Martin was working on his horse and told him about Sheryl. And by all accounts, and I guess there were a lot of folks hanging around, Doug just lost it. He got really upset, almost distraught, someone said. Before the detective said much of anything, he was protesting that he didn't kill either one of them. And the whole story came out. It turns out that Sheryl was pregnant. Doug had wanted her to get an abortion and she wouldn't. She wanted to get married. Doug broke up with Sheryl, and went back to Jane, and Sheryl was just furious. After Jane was shot, Sheryl was trying to get Doug interested again but he wanted nothing to do with fatherhood."

"Oh my God," I said. This explained what Doug and Sheryl had been so intense about when Jeri and I rode through Lazy Valley Stable on Tuesday.

"There's more," Trish said. "Doug told that detective that Sheryl always rode with a twenty-two pistol in her saddlebags. And that he had wondered if maybe Sheryl shot Jane."

"Oh my God," I said again and carried the phone into the bedroom so that Mac could not overhear me.

"Someone said that the detective took Doug in for more questioning. There's talk that maybe Sheryl shot Jane and Doug shot Sheryl. Me, I can't picture Doug shooting anyone."

"Me either," I said.

"But there's another thing," Trish said. "Guess what I saw as I rode in?"

"I can't imagine." I was beginning to feel like Alice in Wonderland.

"It was just getting dark and I noticed a light in the window of this little employee house at the back of the ranch that's been empty for a week. The barn help guy quit and moved out. So I glance that way as I ride by and guess who I saw?"

"Who?"

"Ross and Tammi," Trish said triumphantly. "Sitting at the table eating something."

"Oh my God," I said. I knew I was getting repetitive. "What in the world would they be doing there? Did they see you?"

"I doubt it," Trish said. "It was pretty dark and I'm on a black horse. The house sits about fifty feet from the ranch road. We didn't make any noise. I'm pretty sure they didn't see me. But I do have an idea what they might be doing there."

"What's that?"

"I've been at Lazy Valley almost five years," Trish said. "And Juli has gone through quite a few trainers during that time. Ross used to work for her, you know."

"Now that you mention it, I do kind of remember that," I said.

"Juli smokes a lot of pot," Trish said bluntly. "And I'm pretty sure she bought it from Ross. He used to show up out here from time to time, even after he quit working for her. I've seen him out here in the last few months. He was always talking to Juli. I have the feeling she might be pretty sympathetic to him getting busted for growing pot."

"I see," I said. And I did. Lots of people in Santa Cruz County were very much on the side of the pot growers. "So you think Juli might have decided to hide them out?"

"That's what it looks like to me," Trish said. "There's so many horses out here, and so many coming and going, nobody would notice a couple more. And Ross and Tammi were headed in this direction when I saw them."

"It makes sense," I said. "Though I can't imagine what their plan is. They can't hide there forever."

"Maybe they don't have a plan," Trish said. "I don't recall either one of them being real bright."

"Not the sharpest knives in the drawer," I agreed.

"I've got to go," Trish said. "Thanks for checking on me."

"You're welcome. Any time." I hung up with a sigh. Now I had a lot more information that I should probably tell Jeri. Who was probably grilling Doug Martin at this very moment.

I glanced at the dark outside the window. Windy slaps of rain were spattering the pane. I took a sip of margarita and an appreciative sniff of the stew-laden air. And I turned off the phone. This could all wait until tomorrow morning. I'd had enough for one day. I was taking a break.

*C*hapter 17

JERI WARD PULLED IN MY driveway at eight the next morning, right as I was feeding my horses. The storm had blown through overnight and the sky was washed and blue. I dumped the last flake of hay into Sunny's feeder, and waved at Jeri to come on up to the little house.

"I've got lots to tell you," I said, as we crossed the porch.

Jeri was holding a paper cup of coffee and had the resolutely awake look of the very tired and highly caffeinated.

"Were you out late?" I asked sympathetically.

"Uh-huh. This second homicide makes this case a big, big deal. We questioned Doug Martin for several hours. He hasn't got an alibi for the time of either murder, as close as we can pinpoint it. We think Sheryl Silverman was killed sometime Tuesday afternoon. She left on her trail ride about two o'clock. That's the last anyone admits to seeing her. Doug Martin says he went back to Jane Kelly's house and took care of her dogs and ate a solitary dinner. He was only slightly surprised at not hearing from Sheryl, he says. He figured she just went home to her own place. The first he knew she might be missing was yesterday morning when he got to the stable."

"What does he say about her being pregnant?"

"How do you know that?" Jeri asked me sharply.

"News travels fast around a boarding stable. As far as I can tell, a lot of people overheard Doug getting upset when you showed up out there."

"Yeah, there were a lot of spectators," Jeri said. "I tried to get him out of there, but he didn't want to go."

"So the news traveled," I said. "At least among horse people. It sounds to me like Doug really spilled the beans."

"He was pretty upset," Jeri said. "I think he thought we were going to arrest him."

"Did he seem surprised when you told him Sheryl was dead?"

"He did. Shocked."

"But he would have to act shocked, even if he killed her." I sighed. "So he admitted that she was pregnant?"

"Yep. He pretty much couldn't stop talking. He said that Sheryl Silverman getting pregnant was a problem for him. He did not want the obligations of fatherhood. He's quite clear on that. Sheryl insisted she would keep the baby. She wanted them to get married. Doug says he broke up with her and went back to Jane. He was still trying to convince her to get an abortion. He also says that it crossed his mind that Sheryl might have shot Jane. She usually carried a twenty-two pistol in her saddlebags. My guys are right now checking to see if that gun could have killed Jane Kelly."

"Do you think Doug killed Sheryl?" I asked.

"He's the likely suspect if you go by the book. He's got a clear motive and no alibi. But I'm not ready to arrest him yet. We've got a lot of ground to cover first."

"Speaking of that…" And I told Jeri what Trish had told me about Ross and Tammi.

Even as I finished up, Jeri was getting to her feet. "I'm headed over there," she said.

"There's more. You know that guy with the white dog? Well, he's the one who's been blocking the trails. And I think he may have an irrational hatred of horse people." And I repeated the story that Riva had told me. "That guy's house is the closest place to the spot where Sheryl was shot. And he's just a short ways from where Jane was shot. Not to mention, I think Jane turned back when she met one of his little barriers. Maybe she actually ran into him. I know Jane. If she'd seen him blocking the trails, she would have given him an earful."

"Bill Waters is on my list of people to talk to today," Jeri said. "Anything more, Gail?"

"Not really," I said.

I watched Jeri move purposefully toward my door and felt a little niggle of misgiving. At some level I wanted to be going with her. I wanted to help solve this mystery. I wanted the darkness that hung over the ridge blown away like mist in the sunshine. I wanted to DO something.

Jeri's car drove down my driveway. Mac emerged from the house and began throwing a ball for Star. Even Freckles, spurred on by the puppy, occasionally did some fetching. The little black scruffy ball of fur dodged between Freckles's legs and ran pell-mell after the ball. Mac laughed with delight. I watched and tried to feel the joy in the moment. Tried to let go of this seething need to "do." But it wouldn't let me alone.

There was no peace in my heart and my mind raced with questions. Half an hour later I'd cooked breakfast for Mac and Blue and was feeling no more settled. Mac had arranged to take Star over to his best friend's house to play. Blue had agreed to drive him there. As they headed towards the door I said to Blue, "I might go out for a while. I'll be back this afternoon."

Blue gave me a quizzical look, but said nothing, as was his way. My husband was not an interfering sort, and mostly kept his thoughts to himself.

When Mac and Blue had disappeared I sat down on the porch and stared at the ridge, which sparkled in the fresh sunlight. There was a half-fledged idea in my mind. Perhaps it wasn't a very smart idea. But I had the inescapable urge to do something, and I didn't think there was much point in my driving over to Lazy Valley Stable to see what was going on. I'd only be a nuisance. But there was one place I could go that nobody could stop me from going. The center of the mystery. The ridge.

What Blue would make of this I didn't like to think. But I had an idea. It had come to me when I contemplated just how well I knew the trails. Surely this knowledge could be used to my advantage. If someone was out there shooting people, a hidden watcher might eventually see this person. And there were many places to hide.

The word "hide" had bounced in my mind with odd emphasis, and then I got it. The poacher's blind. The poacher's blind sat high in a tree near the Lookout. There was a chain ladder leading up to a screened platform. It was impossible to tell if anyone was in the blind from the ground. Presumably it had been built to shoot deer.

If I waited in that blind, I might see people on the trails when they did not know they were being observed. And I might learn something. The question was, how to get to the blind? If I rode there I was obviously putting myself at some risk. People on horses were easy to spot. And so far the shooter had targeted riders—for what reason we didn't know. I would be extremely vulnerable if I rode. Also, tying Sunny near the blind would be a dead giveaway that someone was there.

I could hike. Hiking had many advantages. I could be quiet and watchful and would perhaps spot others before they saw me. I could hide in the brush and maybe be unnoticed if I came upon anyone else. But I could not move fast in the case of danger. I was not going to be able to outrun anyone. If I ran into the shooter I would have no defenses, as I did not plan on some sort of western shoot-out scenario. And it would take me an hour to hike to the blind and an hour to hike home.

But there was one other possibility. The thought of Buddy's camper had brought it to my mind. I could drive my four-wheel-drive pickup up the logging road and park it on a log deck near the Lookout. It would take me all of five minutes to hike to the blind from there. And once I was hidden in the blind there would be nothing to show I was there.

Would I see anything useful? Probably not. But there was a chance. It was better than doing nothing. And I would be likely to see anyone who was out on the trails. Most people who hiked or rode made for the Lookout. The view over the bay was spectacular and a destination for most if not all trips along the ridge. So the chances were I would see whoever was out there.

I didn't stop to think about it further. Putting a bottle of water, a small picnic blanket, and my pistol in my daypack, and my cell phone and a camera in my pockets, I headed out to the truck. For lack of a better idea, I was going to hide out on the ridge.

Chapter 18

THE TRUCK BOUNCED AND JOLTED up the rutted dirt road full of potholes. I gritted my teeth and tried not to feel too apprehensive. No one was going to shoot at me in this vehicle, I reassured myself. But I didn't feel too sure about that.

Around me the hills rolled away, empty and serene. I saw two does browsing in the pampas grass meadow. A rabbit hopped across the turf where Buddy's camper was once parked. But the noise of the diesel engine drowned out the sounds of the woods and I was aware that there could be much happening that was lost to me. I did not see any other human travelers—but that did not mean that they weren't there.

I passed the big madrone on the bend and the road tended more steeply uphill. In another minute I would reach the wide place I was thinking of, an old log deck very near the top of the ridge. Here I planned to park the truck and go on foot.

The engine growled with effort as the truck climbed and rocked its way forward. Anyone in the woods right now would know exactly where I was. I sighed. Maybe this wasn't such a clever idea.

The level width of the old log deck appeared on the right, grassy and grown-in. Beyond stretched a vista of rolling hills, blue-green in the distance, tossing like tumbled waves up to the crest of the coastal mountains. I parked the truck and got out, relieved at the sudden silence. For a long while I just stood and listened.

All seemed as usual. The rustle of quail in the brush, the flash and squawk of a blue jay through the trees, the normal noises of the woods and scrub.

Shouldering my pack, I locked the truck and headed up the hill. By my reckoning I was very close to the Lookout clearing, and the hunter's blind. It should only take me five minutes to get there.

I trudged up the slope, glad that I had not elected to walk the whole way. My truck would be invisible to anyone at the Lookout, and even if someone passed by it while riding or hiking this road, they would have no way of knowing that its driver was hiding in the blind.

I was in the redwoods now, and the dazzle of light ahead told me that the Lookout bluff lay just beyond this grove. I walked as quietly as I could, pausing every few steps to look and listen. I wanted to be aware of any other visitors to the Lookout before they were aware of me.

Stepping softly through the shadows underneath the dark redwoods, I peered ahead at the bare clearing. A small breeze riffled through thin stalks of brown dead grass at the edge of the bluff. Beyond that empty space opened up in a blue dazzle of sky and sea. The distant horizon showed the thin line of land curving around the deep aquamarine crescent of the bay. Tumbled coastal hills rolled down to the water. As always the view made me catch my breath. Even such an errand as I was on could not rob this place of its inherent drama.

I stared, waiting, watching, listening. I could see no figures anywhere; I could hear no voices. The Lookout appeared to be deserted. Cautiously I stepped out of the shadows and walked down the road to the clearing.

I reached the crown of the bluff and halted. My eyes shot to the right and scanned up the big oak tree to the hunter's blind, a screened platform in the first fork of the trunk, about twenty feet off the ground. A ladder made out of chain hung from the platform to the ground. I made my way towards the ladder.

The blind sat silent above me; I shook the ladder and gave it a hard tug. It seemed solid. Once again I looked around. No one to be seen. I put my hands on the metal rung above my head and stepped up onto the ladder.

Hand over hand, one step at a time, I climbed slowly up the ladder. It swung wildly with my weight and I found it hard to keep my balance. I kept my concentration steady; I did not look down, just focused on gripping hard and pulling up one rung at a time. And in a minute I heaved myself onto the plywood platform and looked around.

Nothing. Dusty, bare wood. No trash, no gear of any kind. The screen around the platform was of woven willow. It looked sturdy and well supported. I could see easily through the gaps, but knew from riding past the blind that those below could not see me. I had taken the precaution of wearing brown, so felt pretty sure I was invisible. I settled myself as comfortably as I could, facing the Lookout bluff and waited.

And waited. Little spatters of sunlight filtered through the branches and touched my skin. I could see dust motes floating in the air. Outside the blind, jays squawked and squirrels chattered from time to time. I could smell the rich earthy smell of redwood duff from the nearby grove of trees. The clearing I was watching remained deserted. And yet I felt reasonably confident that any-one who was on the trails was likely to aim for the Lookout.

I waited and watched. Shifted from time to time to get comfort-able. The sunlight grew stronger. From where I sat I could see the shining blue of the bay and the open dazzle of the sky…in bits through the woven screen. I stared at a red-tail hawk making big ascending circles as he caught a thermal. I wondered how long I would sit here before something happened. And then it hit me.

This was the life I had been asking for. This, just this, was what I proposed to choose over resuming my career as a horse vet. Sit-ting and watching. Watching the light change in the sky. Watching the seasons in my garden. Watching the wild creatures. This was it. This was the whole deal.

The thought almost made me laugh out loud. Be careful what you ask for. Holding still and watching, just being, sounds easy, but in practice not so much, as those who meditate can attest. In theory one might watch the light change and the shadows lengthen. In practice, one combats boredom and sore joints, as I was doing now.

I stretched each leg in turn and peered through the screen. The clearing remained empty and quiet; sparse, dried brown grass flickered in the intermittent breeze, which seemed to be rising. A rabbit hopped into view and then jumped back into a patch of thistles. I wondered if I'd been here an hour.

Glancing back again, I stiffened. Movement in the grass at the edge of the clearing near the trail that led to Moon Valley resolved itself into a gray-brown cat-like form. In another moment the tufted ears and short tail of the lynx let me know that this was a bobcat, a common dweller in these hills. Nonetheless I watched, fascinated. Despite the fact that I had seen bobcats hundreds of times since living here, I never lost interest in observing them.

This bobcat was a large one and very spotted. The white belly and legs were leopard-like with black dots. I had seen bobcats of an overall golden brown like a cougar, and even one with pronounced white socks on its back legs like a domestic cat. But I had never seen one either this large or this spotted.

The bobcat hesitated and raised its head to sniff the air, looking carefully about, very much as I had done when I entered the clearing. The long side whiskers, somewhat like a Fu Manchu mustache, quivered slightly. Then the cat walked forward confidently, with that peculiar high-in-the-rear-end gait so characteristic of these lynxes. Bobcats tended to move with confidence, in my experience, not seeming very afraid of anything, including humans. This bobcat stalked calmly across the open bluff, looked back once over its shoulder, and vanished down the trail that led to the old reservoir.

I took a deep gulp of air; I hadn't realized I'd been holding my breath. And then I heard voices.

I held perfectly still and strained to listen. A male voice and a female voice, it sounded like. Coming from the direction the bobcat had come. Coming up the trail that led to Moon Valley.

And in another moment I saw two mounted horsemen scramble up the last steep bit of hill and emerge into the open. I blinked. Surely that was Tammi and Ross.

Tammi wore a halter top; I could see her tattoos from here. Ross had a ball cap on, but I was sure it was him. They rode two sorrel horses; I did not know their horses well enough to have any idea if these were their own animals or not. But it was certainly Ross and Tammi.

They parked their horses side by side in front of the view. I could hear their voices, but frustratingly, I could not make out a word of what they were saying. At moments it looked as though they were arguing. I watched intently the entire time they sat and talked, but could see or hear nothing of interest. Neither had a backpack or saddlebags, I noted.

Eventually they wheeled their horses and rode toward me. It looked as though they planned to take the logging road. In a moment they would pass right by my tree. My heart began beating harder. Even though I felt sure I was hidden, the thought of being discovered by these two made my gut tense. Who knew just how much they were on the run from? I strained to catch what Tammi was saying.

"Dammit, Ross, we can't hide there forever. That detective was out there this morning looking for us. Juli's going to cave under the pressure. It's just luck we were back behind the barn when that stupid girl cop drove in. Otherwise she might have caught us. We need to get out of there."

"You got any good ideas just how to do that, Tam? You think we ought to steal Juli's car?" Ross's voice was harsh.

And then they were past me and I could no longer make out words.

Hmmm…looked like Jeri had failed at picking up Ross and Tammi. But apparently they were still hiding out at Lazy Valley

Stable. Nothing in what I had heard told me whether they were hiding there solely because of being busted for pot growing, or if they were involved in the shootings.

I shifted my weight and crossed my legs. At least I had seen something worth noting. I would just hang out here awhile longer.

Time passed. The wind rocked the branches of my tree. For a while I lay on my back and gazed upward, watching the shifting patterns of green leaves against blue sky. From time to time I rolled on my side and peered through the screen, but there was nothing to be seen. Other than a haze growing over the ocean, which promised that the weather might be changing again.

I watched the oak leaves dance across the sky, green against blue, a brilliant kaleidoscope. Rolling over, I peered through the screen. Something moved right below me and I nearly let out a startled squawk. A big buck was walking up the trail, just passing my blind.

The buck seemed unaware of me; I watched him browse idly on some ceanothus branches that overhung the trail. He had odd-shaped antlers—very wide, like a cow's horns, and a dark blaze down his face. His nose was black and shiny and the white under his tail flashed as he flicked it upward from time to time. Suddenly his head came up and he looked back over his shoulder. In another moment he bounded into the redwoods beside the trail and disappeared.

Now what had startled the buck? I waited and watched. And in another few seconds a hiker came into view. The thickset guy with the yellow Lab. Hiking steadily up the trail, the Lab wagging his tail and huffing a little. They both passed under my tree without looking up. The hiker glanced at the Lookout view but kept moving, taking the logging road back down the hill. As before, he carried a machete and wore a pack.

Well, Brandon Carter had said this guy hiked up here all the time. Something about him was familiar, but I just couldn't place what it was.

I stretched my legs and arms in turn and wondered how much longer I wanted to stay here. Judging by the light, it was about noon. The sky was starting to cloud up. I took a drink of water and settled down to wait some more.

Crossing my arms behind my head, I lay down on my back and gazed upward at the leaves, waving against the drifting clouds. The wind hummed in the branches. Steadily the humming grew louder, and I suddenly sat up straight. That was not the wind. It was an engine.

A sharp, fairly high-pitched engine. And in another moment I was sure. That was the noise of a dirt bike, rapidly approaching up the logging road.

The whine of the motor grew louder and louder, drowning out all other sounds. I stared in the direction of the logging road and saw the motorcycle emerge from the redwoods, shrieking its noisy song. The rider had a beard; it was clearly the same guy I'd seen before. He blasted across the clearing and spun a donut in the middle, tearing up the ground and raising a cloud of dust in the air. Nice.

Pulling up in front of the view, the bearded guy cut the engine and laid the bike down. For a second he glanced around the clearing, and then looked over his shoulder, right at the tree I was in. Purposefully he started in that direction.

Shit. Oh shit. It had never occurred to me that others might climb up in this blind from time to time. For all I knew, this noisy biker might have built the blind. Hadn't Jeri said that he lived in the big subdivision?

My heart thumped a pounding rhythm as I watched the hiker stride toward me. I fingered the pistol in the pack at my side. Sure. I could hardly go pointing a gun at someone who had done nothing worse than climb into the blind, not knowing I was there. But the thought of being trapped in the blind with this particular individual made the hair rise on the back of my neck.

Something in his very energy was unsettling. His stride, the carriage of his head, his facial expression—all were arrogant, as if the rest of the world should get out of his way. I remembered the several times he had blasted by me on his motorcycle while I was out riding, and what Jane had said about him. Even the idly destructive circular donut dug into the dusty ground of the Lookout was testament to this guy's obvious jerkdom. At a guess he was a rich kid who had never learned to respect anything, grown to be a lazy man who had nothing better to do than tear up the scenery in a noisy fashion. My hand clenched on the butt of the gun.

He was out of my sight now, right underneath the platform. What had Jeri said his name was? Len something. I heard the clink of the chain ladder. Oh shit.

My heart thudded like it would jump out of my chest. I crouched silently, holding the gun, not sure at all what I should do if this guy emerged on the platform. The feeling of the heavy, solid weight of the .357 in my hand was reassuring, but it didn't constitute a plan of action.

For a second there was silence. I strained to hear the noise of the ladder squeaking and clanking. Nothing. The chains did not move. What was he doing?

It would be impossible for anyone to climb the ladder without the chains moving and they were still. What the hell was he doing? It was very quiet. I could see the dirt bike lying on its side in the clearing. I thought I could hear tiny rustling noises from beneath the platform. Crouching silently, I strained to hear or see something.

And then I smelled smoke. For a second my mind reeled. Was he setting the tree on fire? I breathed in deeply. The smoky whiff in the air was plain, and something else. A particular distinct herbal smell. I shook my head. Pot. The guy was smoking pot. Sitting under the tree smoking a joint. I knew it as clearly as if I could see it.

The relief was huge. He wasn't on his way up to the platform, he wasn't setting the woods on fire. Just smoking a joint. I half smiled.

Maybe one that he'd bought from Ross. Perhaps Len was another one of Ross's customers.

This thought brought another flurry of ideas. Could Ross and his pot growing operation have more connections to the shooting deaths in the woods than I had ever supposed? I couldn't imagine what the connections might be, but pot seemed to keep coming up. Trish had said that Juli smoked it and had bought it from Ross. Juli was currently hiding Ross and Tammi. Ross and Tammi's indoor gardening was the source of the mysterious light on the ridge which had puzzled me for months. And now the bearded dirt bike rider who had come close to mowing me down was enjoying a joint while I crouched above him. It all seemed very odd.

More rustling noises from underneath the platform. And then the bearded guy emerged, stretching his arms above his head. I longed to do the same but didn't dare move. I noticed that he had a small daypack on his back, very like my own. Big enough to conceal a pistol.

The man had his back to me now; he was walking away. Headed toward his motorcycle. Once again I was struck by the arrogance of his stride. I could still smell the lingering odor of marijuana.

I watched him walk to his motorcycle, jerk it up off the ground, throw his leg over it, and start the engine. For a second he glanced around and then revved the motor and took off, back wheel spinning in the loose dirt. I sighed and stretched my legs and arms, while the dirt bike disappeared down the trail in a blast of angry sound.

Grateful to see the last of this visitor I scanned idly around the clearing and nearly jumped a foot. Someone was there, standing in the grove of redwood trees where the logging road emerged. Looking very carefully around the bluff. And I knew who that someone was.

Chapter 19

BRANDON CARTER STOOD IN THE shadows of the redwood grove, his rifle cradled in his arms. For a second he squatted and peered at the ground in front of him, then he stood up and looked carefully around the clearing. Every inch of his demeanor proclaimed he was searching for something. The question was what?

After a moment he walked forward slowly, turning his head from side to side like a satellite dish scanning for a signal. At one point his eyes rested on the blind where I crouched, holding my breath. For some odd reason I had the notion he could see through the screen and knew where I was hiding.

Brandon kept walking, glancing down from time to time at the ground in front of him. He was tracking something, I thought. I just hoped it wasn't me.

Brandon strolled quietly across the clearing, his eyes shifting downward from time to time. Eventually he stopped, about twenty feet from the tree where I was hidden. He looked down and then up. For a long moment he seemed to meet my eyes through the screen.

I stayed frozen, holding my breath. But I had the inescapable conviction that Brandon guessed I was hidden in the blind.

Brandon Carter's body language remained relaxed. The rifle was carried loosely in his right hand, not pointed at anything. After a minute his gaze shifted from the blind and he looked out over the ocean. One shoulder twitched in what might have been a minuscule shrug. And then Brandon moseyed slowly off in the direction of the trail that led to the reservoir and disappeared from my sight.

Whew. I had no idea what was in Brandon's mind, but I suddenly wanted out of here. I did not want to be trapped by a guy with a rifle.

I hesitated, not wanting to leave the blind until I was sure Brandon was long gone. Wind skimmed through my hair and the air was getting colder. By my reckoning it was midafternoon. Time to go home.

I stared around the clearing and could see and hear nothing. Just the wind in the trees. I scooted to the edge of the platform and froze. Motion from the direction of the logging road—something was coming.

The movement shortly became a bicycle. A bicycle being pedaled by a guy with a shiny bald head. Oh shit. As the form came closer I was sure that it was Buddy. I immediately pictured his odd eyes with the white rims and quickly tucked my feet out of sight.

Buddy pedaled on, crossing the clearing and stopping in front of the view. He carried a small pack on his back, and wore ragged jeans and a T-shirt. Taking a drink from a water bottle hung from his pack, he glanced around the clearing in an idle way, and then swung the bike around and pedaled towards my tree. In a minute it became obvious that he was headed down toward the pretty trail. I watched him disappear down the hill.

Now that was one guy I really did not want to meet up here.

I slithered to the edge of the platform, grabbed the ladder, and began to lower myself. I was done. I wanted out of here. Hand over hand, one step at a time, I descended the swaying chain ladder until my feet touched the ground. Heaving a sigh of relief, I glanced quickly around the deserted clearing and headed off in the direction of my truck and the logging road. I was going home.

Twenty minutes later I pulled in my own driveway. I had seen no one on my return trip, and my truck appeared undisturbed, though it seemed to me that there were unfamiliar footprints around it. More than one set, I thought.

Blue and Mac were home, both hanging out in the little house. Blue was playing his pipes and Mac was immersed in a book on physics, one of his favorite subjects. Freckles and Star were asleep on the floor. Everybody seemed happy to see me; nobody asked where I'd been. Good.

I went over to the main house and made a sandwich and a cup of tea and sat down on the porch. The wind riffled across our little hollow in the hills, rustling the drooping sunflowers and the dry bean vines on the garden tepee. Whirling leaves whipped through the air. Fall was really here.

I took a sip of tea and squinted through the steam at the distant ridgeline. There, silhouetted against the cloudy sky, was the grove of redwoods that stood near the Lookout. The Lookout bluff and the oak tree with the blind were hidden behind the tall eucalyptus trees on the ridge trail in the foreground, but I knew exactly where the blind was in relation to the redwoods I could see. Less than an hour ago I had been there, hidden on that platform, watching the woods.

The notion of here and there, now and then, still fascinated me, even embroiled in the mystery of the trails as I was. I sat on my porch and sipped my tea and reviewed the hours I had waited in the blind. I'd seen a number of things—I just wasn't sure what they all meant.

Sandwich eaten and tea drunk, I went into the house to call Jeri Ward.

She answered on the first ring. "Hi Gail. What's new?"

"I've been watching the woods. I saw some people."

"You've been what?"

"Watching up in the woods."

"What are you talking about exactly?"

"Jeri, I'd rather not tell you exactly. Do you want to know who I saw?"

There was a moment's silence. Then, "I'll be over there in about an hour. It's better if we talk there."

"All right," I said, and hung up.

I spent the next hour playing with Mac and Star in the new house, while the sky grew darker. Evening was drawing in and it felt like a storm was coming. The light had that odd greenish hue it often got on the brink of blustery weather. Eventually Mac and Blue decided to make tacos for dinner and headed over to the main house to build a fire in the woodstove and begin their cooking. I fed the horses and then waited in the little house for Jeri.

The sight of headlights coming up my driveway caused me to sit up straighter in the rocking chair. Jeri parked her car and strode up the hill at a brisk pace. Looked like she was in a hurry.

I stood up and pulled the sliding glass door. Jeri walked through it talking. "What were you doing, Gail?"

"I was up in the woods, watching," I said. "There's no law that says I can't hang out in the woods."

"Well, it's pretty goddamn dumb," Jeri snapped. "Do you want to be the next victim?"

"I wasn't riding, and no one knew I was there. Besides I thought you guys had decided that Sheryl shot Jane and Doug killed Sheryl."

"Sheryl's gun did not kill Jane, as it turns out. And it looks as though the same gun killed both of them," Jeri said tersely. "We haven't arrested Doug Martin. There is still the distinct possibility that these shootings were random."

"Just happened to be two women on horseback? Who happened to both be dating the same guy?"

"I know," Jeri sighed. "I just got done interviewing Bill Waters, the guy with the white dog. He is hostile enough to take out a whole boatload of horse people. He went on and on about how the horses tear up the ground and so forth. He admits to blocking the trails and siccing his dog on riders. And he says he did not hear the shot that killed Sheryl, though he was at home with no alibi on Tuesday afternoon. Neither does he have an alibi for Saturday afternoon when Jane was shot. So he's definitely on my radar."

"How about Ross and Tammi?"

"I went out to Lazy Valley to pick them up, but the owner swore she'd never seen them. My next step is to get a search warrant."

"I think you'd better do that."

"Why's that?" Jeri's eyes shot to mine.

"Well, do you want to hear what I saw up in the woods?"

"Sure."

"Ross and Tammi for one thing." And I recounted what I had seen and heard.

"Now that is very interesting," Jeri said. "What else did you see?"

"Well, a bobcat and a buck. Also Brandon Carter and that hiker with the yellow Lab. And the bearded guy that rides the dirt bike. Len something. And Buddy."

"Buddy?" Jeri's spine stiffened. "The guy with the camper?"

"Yeah, him. He was on a bike. I didn't see the camper, though I went right past the spot where it used to be parked."

Jeri gave me a funny look, but said nothing.

"Have you thought about the way pot just keeps coming into this?" I asked her. "First Ross and his pot growing scheme and Jane turning him in, then Jane gets shot, and Juli supposedly buys pot from Ross and is now hiding him, and that dirt bike guy sat down and smoked a joint."

"You saw this?" Jeri asked.

"More or less," I said. "Just don't ask."

"All right," Jeri said slowly, "but don't you do anything dumb."

"Right," I said.

"I think I will get a warrant and go search Lazy Valley," Jeri said, getting to her feet. "I need to talk to Ross Hart. Thanks for the info." And she walked to the door. With her thumb on the handle, she looked back at me. "Be careful, Gail. I mean it."

"Right," I said again. "I will." I thought, but didn't say, that I didn't plan on falling out of the blind and I ought to be just fine. I was pretty sure Jeri would not have seen it the way I did.

Chapter 20

AT TEN THE NEXT MORNING I was on my way to the blind. Blue had taken Mac to the homeschool group, which met on Tuesdays and Fridays. After that Blue was going to a bagpipe lesson and then picking Mac up again. No one would wonder where I was until midafternoon. I had plenty of time for some observation on the ridge.

I did not question why I was so determined to do this. I already knew that Jeri, and no doubt Blue, would think it qualified as dumb. But yesterday had convinced me that I might, indeed, see some things that would provide useful information towards solving this mystery. And I was determined that it would be solved. I wanted to ride my yellow horse on many more pleasant trail rides. I did not want to be forever afraid to be out in the woods.

I drove slowly up the logging road under gray skies, reflecting that I would, indeed, be afraid if I were riding my horse right now. The feeling that someone might be watching me, sighting a gun on me, was causing me to tense up, even in the truck. I would feel a thousand times more vulnerable on my horse.

This thought brought another to mind. Was this shooter targeting equestrians just because they were on horses? Was he specifically targeting women on horses? And if so, why? An irrational distaste for horse traffic? Or something more bizarre? Or was this your typical love triangle with Doug Martin in the center? Somehow I had a hard time believing that.

My instincts shouted that this mystery had to do with the ridge; from the beginning I had felt what seemed like a dark shadow hanging over my beloved trails. It was this that lay at the root of my determination. I wanted to clear the stain on the hills of my home. And the only way to make that happen was to bring the murderer to justice.

I was surprised at the sudden rush of pure fury that seethed through my veins at the thought of a murderer haunting these hills. My jaw clenched and fear almost disappeared in the rush of burning rage. Damn it, this evil beast WAS going to be hunted down as he deserved, and the trails would be free and beautiful again. For fucking sure.

I shook my head, trying to clear my mind of the anger. I needed to pay attention to my surroundings, not get lost in fantasies of revenge. But I was aware of the powerful current that coursed through my body, even as I did my best to pilot the truck carefully up the rough road.

Potholes caused the vehicle to bounce awkwardly; we were crossing the pampas grass meadow now. I looked idly to my right, across the open sandy terrain, dotted with big, rustling clumps of the invasive grass, and suddenly slammed on the brakes. Over in the far corner, half hidden under a tree, I could see something white. It was completely screened from the road, except when seen from this one spot. But I was pretty sure that it was Buddy's camper.

After a minute I let the truck creep forward. I did not feel up to accosting Buddy on my own, nor was I sure that there was much point to it. I had no evidence that Buddy was the culprit. But I would darn sure tell Jeri Ward where that camper was parked.

Up the road I jounced, trying to stay out of the bigger ruts and holes. I went slowly, peering through the windshield, making an effort to be aware of as much as I could despite the loud noise of the diesel engine. But I saw nothing worth noting.

Eventually I reached the logging deck where I had parked

yesterday and stopped the truck in the same spot. With a sigh of relief I turned off the noisy engine.

As soon as I got out of the truck the wind smacked me, fresh and sharp. There was a cool edge to it that said rain was not far away. The fringed tops of the redwoods ahead of me waved briskly as I started up the road, shouldering my pack on my back.

I kept my head down, as strands of my hair brushed across my eyes. Flicking them away with my hand, I kept walking, almost trotting. I was eager to reach the blind and concealment. I felt uncomfortably vulnerable out in the open.

Covering the ground as quickly as I could, I made my way towards the tree with the ladder. I glanced from side to side, but did not pause to reconnoiter and check in with the woods. That could wait until I was hidden. The knife edge of the harsh breeze was making me shiver, even through the thick sweatshirt I wore. I was looking forward to the shelter of the blind.

When I reached the big oak tree, I shook the ladder once to make sure it seemed solid, and reached up for the rungs. The chains swung out awkwardly as I climbed, but I was prepared for this after yesterday, and just kept hauling myself up, hand over hand. Once I got to the platform, I heaved myself over the edge and rolled onto the floor. Right on top of a pair of boots.

What the hell? I looked upward and met the blue, blue eyes of Brandon Carter.

Oh shit. My heart dropped as if it were in a falling elevator. I could hardly catch my breath. From my completely vulnerable position on the floor of the blind I croaked, "What the hell are you doing here?"

Brandon smiled. "Just what you were doing yesterday, or so I assume. Watching the woods. Seeing what there is to see."

I sat up and stared at him. "How do you know I was here yesterday?"

"I saw your truck and tracked you up here. I knew you'd gone to this blind; that's where your tracks went. I hid in the brush over there and watched you climb down after the camper dude rode off on his bicycle."

"Oh you did." I could think of nothing appropriate to say. There was no earthly reason for me to protest against Brandon's presence here. I had no claim to the blind. I had seen him yesterday and had wondered if he was tracking me. Brandon's woods skills were clearly a bit superior to mine. I had certainly not realized that he'd watched me climb down from the blind. Nor had I looked carefully at the ground before I'd climbed the ladder a minute ago. If I had, no doubt I would have noticed his bootprints on the dusty ground.

Should I leave? Would he let me?

Brandon watched the thoughts cross my mind.

"You can stay or go. It's no matter to me," he said.

"What are you going to do?"

"Watch. Just like you did. I thought you had a pretty good idea. What did you see?"

I stared at him. Was I going to throw in here? Did I have any reason to trust this guy?

Well, Jeri had said that his gun had not killed Jane, so presumably not Sheryl either. That was one thing. And for some reason I liked him. I wasn't sure what that meant. But still, why would he hide in this blind to catch the murderer if he WAS the murderer?

Of course, he could be hiding in the blind in order to shoot someone. I could see his rifle resting on the floor. But in that case, why not shoot me as I strolled across the clearing, oblivious to his presence? No, I did not think Brandon was the murderer. Was he then an ally? I still wasn't sure.

"I saw Buddy, the camper guy, and you," I said dubiously, knowing he already knew that.

"And you saw that guy with the beard on his dirt bike," Brandon remarked, his arms crossed over his chest, his very blue eyes meeting my gaze steadily. "I watched him ride away from here."

"Yeah," I said, still dubious. Brandon's crossed arms and slightly cocked head looked defensive but not hostile. I still wasn't sure where he was coming from.

"Did you see the guy with the yellow Lab?" he asked.

"Yeah," I said again. "And Ross and Tammi," I added. "On horseback."

There was a moment of silence while Brandon assimilated this. "That trainer and his girlfriend from the boarding stable," he said at last. "The ones who got busted for growing pot."

"That would be them."

"I heard the sheriffs were looking for them."

"They are."

"And you're friends with Sergeant Jeri Ward. Did you mention you'd seen those two?"

"Yep."

Brandon was quiet a long moment. "Wonder if she picked them up."

"That I don't know. I think they're hiding out at Lazy Valley."

"The rich girl's boarding stable."

"You mean Juli?"

"Juli's got a lot of money," Brandon said quietly. "I know her from way back."

I found this interesting. Brandon, the tough, twentyish poacher, knew Juli Barnes, the wealthy, fortyish owner of Lazy Valley Stable. I wondered exactly how he knew her, but didn't want to ask.

Taking a deep breath, I realized I was starting to relax a little. I hadn't exactly made a conscious decision, but somehow I was beginning to trust that Brandon and I were on the same side. I scooted back until my spine rested against the wall of the blind opposite the side where he sat. Maybe I wouldn't leave immediately.

Brandon watched my shift; then looked from me to the outside world and back again at me.

"So who do you think did it?" I asked him.

"You mean shot those women?"

"Yes."

"If I knew, do you think I'd be sitting here?"

"But do you have any thoughts?"

Brandon met my eyes and for the first time, I thought I could read his emotion. Confused.

"Not really," he said at last. "I know it wasn't me. And I damn sure plan to catch whoever it is and get them stopped. Permanently."

"I feel more or less the same way," I said. "Do you think this is about horses? Women on horses in particular."

Now Brandon looked curious. "I dunno," he said. "I've had the thought. Some kook who doesn't like women on horses. Or obsesses on them. Or something like that."

"So, anybody come to mind that fits that description?"

Brandon shook his head slowly. "Not really. But there wouldn't be any way of telling, maybe. I once knew a guy who seemed really normal. And then he went home one night and shot his girlfriend because he thought she was cheating on him. He seemed like a nice guy. I never thought he'd do something like that."

"Yeah," I said, thinking of Doug Martin, who seemed like such a nice guy. Both women who had been shot had been involved with him. And yet I couldn't believe Doug was a killer—he seemed like such a "nice guy." Hmmm...

Suddenly Brandon stiffened and I saw his gaze go to the screen. I turned my head to follow his eyes and he raised a finger to his lips. In a moment I saw what he had seen. A big white dog was bounding up the trail that led to the reservoir.

I stared; Brandon stared. I knew that dog. It was the white standard poodle that lived in the blue house near the trail. The dog that routinely chased horses at the behest of his owner. What had Jeri said the guy's name was? Bill Waters, I thought. Cocky-looking dark-haired guy. Riva from the Red Barn had said he was the one blocking the trails, and that he had threatened her. Jeri had said that he sounded willing to take out a "whole boatload of horse people."

The dog ran on up the trail toward the Lookout clearing. I stiffened. Coming through the trees behind the white dog was a human figure. Stocky, dark-haired, moving fast. Small dayback on his back. Definitely Bill Waters. I'd only seen him a few times, but coupled with the fact that he accompanied the dog, which I did recognize, I was pretty sure it was him.

My eyes went to Brandon, who again raised his finger to his lips. And we both watched.

Man and dog approached the Lookout at a fast clip, looking as if they were going somewhere with a purpose. Bill Waters wore a dark T-shirt and black running shorts. He barely glanced over one shoulder at the view—a whited-out sky and ocean, mixed with grayish clouds—before turning to take the trail which led past the blind and on down the hill to the pretty trail. The dog circled around him once and then took the lead as they moved through the trees. In another minute they were out of sight.

"Do you know that guy?" I whispered, once they were gone.

"I know who he is," Brandon said. "Lives in a blue house near that trail," and he pointed at the trail the guy had come up. "That's one guy who doesn't like horses."

"I know," I said. "Do you see him out in the woods?"

"Every once in awhile," Brandon said. "He doesn't talk to me."

We both pondered on that awhile. The wind rocked the oak tree; the sky seemed to be getting darker. I wondered if it was going to start spitting rain. I wasn't sure I planned to stay up here in a storm. I felt pretty damn cold already.

A low rumble in the distance that sounded like thunder made me flinch. I pulled the hood up on my sweatshirt. And then I froze. Voices. Once again I stiffened and my eyes shot to the screen. Brandon was already looking where I was looking. Neither of us bothered to shush the other. We were both watching.

In another moment I was aware that the voices were male and coming from the direction of the trail that led to Lazy Valley. I strained to see through the cracks in the screen, and was rewarded by the sight of a buckskin horse emerging from the brush. The rider was immediately recognizable. Jonah Wakefield, wearing his trademark black duster and felt hat. It took me a minute, but I realized the guy behind him, riding what I was sure was Dolly, was Doug Martin. The two men were talking, but as before, when Ross and Tammi had ridden up here yesterday, they parked themselves in front of the view, and though I could sometimes hear their voices over the noise of the wind, I could not make out the words.

Brandon and I looked at each other and kept quiet. I tried to decide by watching the men's body language if they were allies or adversarial. It was hard to tell. But in a very short while they stopped talking. Jonah jerked his chin at Doug and rode off on the trail that led to the reservoir.

Doug took the trail that led down the hill, past the blind and on to the pretty trail—the same trail Bill Waters and his white dog had taken. I watched Doug's face as he rode by the blind. Set and cold—a stern expression. I hadn't a clue what lay beneath it. I was used to seeing Doug with a charming smile. The man riding Dolly was not a Doug that I was familiar with.

When Doug had disappeared Brandon glanced at me. "I know who the trainer guy is," he said. "Who's the other guy?"

"Doug Martin," I said softly. "Guy who was the boyfriend of both the women who got shot?"

"Both?"

"Yeah, both. Sequentially, more or less."

"Doesn't that make him suspect number one?"

"Yeah, I think it does."

"And here he is, up in the woods. I noticed he had saddlebags."

"He did, didn't he. And I think they were the same ones that belonged to the second woman who was shot. Sheryl. And by his own account, she always carried a twenty-two pistol in them. I wonder if it's there now?"

"Is that right?" Brandon's whole body looked intent, like a cat that has spotted a gopher in the grass. I could almost see his tail twitching. He stared off in the direction Doug had taken, every sense on the alert.

I shifted my gaze and combed the Lookout clearing. All quiet. And then my eyes bounced back to the logging road. The road passed through a grove of redwoods before it reached the open ground. Was that something moving in the shadows? Or just the tree branches waving in the wind?

The branches of the oak tree I was in rocked and rustled; I strained to see and hear over the gusts that were sweeping in from the ocean. The very air seemed to be turning gray. Dark redwoods swayed and shifted at the edge of the clearing, but surely that was something moving at ground level. Something dark. With a light spot at the top.

I blinked. A horse and rider were coming through the trees, about to emerge into the open. And I was pretty sure it was Trish and Coal. Dark horse, rider with bright sun-gold hair.

I took a deep breath and turned toward Brandon, meaning to motion to him so that he would notice Trish. But his focus on the trail that led down the hill was rigidly intent. I raised my hand to signal him, and suddenly things started happening so fast I could hardly follow them.

In a split second Brandon went from a silent statue to a full-on bellow of rage. Leaping to his feet, gun in hand, still looking down the trail, he shouted at the top of his lungs, "Drop it, you bastard!"

And pointing his rifle in the direction he'd been staring, he pulled the trigger.

Crack! And then another loud bang. The noise rang in my ears even as my eyes shot back to Trish. Coal was spinning, clearly spooked; Trish was on him and trying to regain control. And I got it.

I stood up and screamed as loud as I could. "Run, Trish! Run! Get out of here!"

Trish must have heard me because she quit fighting Coal and let him wheel around and bolt back down the road, as he clearly wanted to do. In another second she was out of sight. And Brandon was halfway down the ladder.

I didn't stop to think if this was a good idea. I just followed him.

*C*hapter 21

BY THE TIME I HAD SCRAMBLED down the wildly swinging ladder, Brandon was a distant figure pelting down the hill. I headed after him as fast as I could, my pack thumping me hard on the back with every stride. Sticks snapped under my feet and I tried to keep my focus divided between Brandon and the trail as I ran downhill on the uneven ground.

I had no idea who Brandon was chasing, but I was pretty damn sure it was the author of that second shot. I was guessing, but I imagined that Brandon had seen or heard something, enough to make him shout and fire his gun. And I thought the something was someone. Someone who shot at Trish. But Trish was okay; I'd seen her galloping the frightened Coal down the hill. Between Brandon's shot, Coal's spook, and my warning, Trish had escaped becoming the next victim.

Running as hard as I could, trying to keep Brandon in sight, I tried to guess who we were after. Doug Martin? Certainly he had just disappeared down this trail on horseback. Were we chasing a mounted rider? Had Doug tried to shoot Trish?

Brandon had reached the juncture with the pretty trail, but he headed left, towards the ridge trail. I did not see Doug anywhere. I pushed myself harder, not wanting to lose sight of Brandon.

But Brandon was younger and more athletic than I was; he was drawing away from me. My heart was pounding and I was already gasping for air. I wasn't going to be able to keep this up very long. At least we were going downhill.

In some corner of my mind I could feel the wind buffet me and the sting of small rain on my cheek. The storm was coming. I kept running.

Down, down, through a tangle of shrubbery, past the three-way trail crossing, still on the ridge trail. I huffed and puffed, my legs churning; I could see Brandon far ahead of me. He was running through the big Monterey pines. And I saw him take the branch trail that led to the landmark tree skeleton.

I charged after him. This trail led steeply downhill and dead-ended behind the big mansions on Storybook Lane. I never rode this way anymore, but I had hiked it a few times in the last few years to look at the landmark tree. If we were chasing Doug, I could not imagine what his plan might be. Gallop through someone's backyard and down the suburban street?

Running and gasping, I struggled to stay upright on the steep slope. My feet wanted to slip forward; I ran faster and faster, letting gravity pull me downhill. The huge trunk of the landmark tree loomed on my right, towering into the dark gray clouds above. I could no longer see Brandon. I just ran.

Down and down, greenness blurred in my peripheral vision; I thought I had almost reached the seasonal pond, dry now, that lay behind the last big house at the end of the road. And a sudden memory popped into my mind. This was the way I had ridden, many years ago, when a wealthy suburbanite had banned me from the subdivision. I had come down this same trail on horseback and ridden up behind the big house at the end of the road, only to have a middle-aged man emerge from the house and scream at me in fury, threatening to call the sheriffs on me, should I ever come through here again. I could still remember his face, contorted with rage. His face…

I was still running, but the gears in my mind were turning faster than my legs could pump. His face was familiar. I knew that face. And suddenly I knew who we were chasing.

The recognition came crashing in as I spotted Brandon's form ahead of me, on the other side of the pond, moving fast toward the grapestake fence that marked the backyard of the house. I didn't have time to draw a breath, much less shout, before the shot rang out. And Brandon dropped to the ground.

Chapter 22

SHIT. OH SHIT. I DROPPED to the ground behind a clump of willows, wrestled my pack off my back, and pulled out the gun. The pistol felt reassuring in my hand, but I hadn't a clue what to do. I could not see who had shot at Brandon. I could, however, see Brandon's form, and he was moving.

He lunged to his feet, but staggered and fell again at the edge of the dried-up pond, about thirty feet from the scrub willow that shielded me. The open bowl of the empty pond lay between us. I could see bright red blood staining his chest.

My heart felt like it was going to leave my body. I stared hard in the direction from which the shot had come. From behind that fence I thought. From the yard of that house. What in the hell was I going to do here?

And a tiny voice said, remember your cell phone.

I dug it out of my pocket, already knowing it wouldn't work. I was not a hundred yards, as the crow flies, from the spot where Jane had been shot. Once again I was at the bottom of this hollow in the hills. There was not going to be a signal. I stared at the screen. Nope. I was on my own.

Wind howled through the tree tops on the ridge, but the hollow where this pond lay was fairly sheltered. Rain spattered fitfully in the gloom. I shivered and then took a deep breath. Time to get centered.

I sighted my pistol in the direction of the fence and waited. With any luck the shooter did not know of my presence here. I had been screened by the brush as I descended the hill. The gunman was after Brandon, who had pursued him. I was unknown, invisible, here behind the willows. I might have a chance. I sighted down the barrel of the gun and waited.

And waited. Brandon wasn't moving. He had fallen face down. I didn't know if he was dead or alive. I felt sure the shooter would be wondering the same thing. I waited.

The wind gusted through the willow branches but other than that the woods were silent. Not a bird chirped, not a lizard rustled in the dry grass. The sudden shot had scared the brush into frozen quiet. I could feel blackberry thorns digging into my knee, but ignored them. I would stay frozen, too. Waiting.

It seemed to take forever, but eventually a head appeared above the fence. Heavy-featured, short light brown hair. The face of a thickset middle-aged man. An ordinary sort of face. The kind of man you might see out walking his dog.

My heart beat a rapid tattoo. This was the face I'd been expecting. The face that had looked oddly familiar. Just a middle-aged man out walking his friendly yellow Lab. But it was the same man who had run me out of here so many years ago. Who lived in this big house at the end of the road and hated horses.

I had never made the connection. Too many years had passed in between. I hadn't known the hiker lived in this house. I'd recognized that his face looked familiar, but that was it.

Slowly the face turned from side to side, scanning the woods. I held absolutely still. And then a gate opened in the fence and the man stepped out, his eyes on Brandon's form. He walked cautiously in that direction. There was a pistol in his hand.

I had a few seconds. Jumbled thoughts raced through my mind. Mac and Blue, right and wrong. But I could see only one course. I sighted carefully down my gun as the heavyset man reached Brandon.

He was lifting his pistol towards Brandon's head, but I was ready. Aiming for the center of that thick body, I held my breath and pulled the trigger.

The recoil knocked my arm back, the crack rang in my ears. He turned his head towards me; I shot again. Bringing the gun back to the center of his body, I shot a third time. Again I centered myself, ready to shoot. But the man collapsed next to Brandon.

I didn't hesitate. Leaping to my feet, I ran toward the two of them. I could see the killer's pistol on the ground near his hand and I kicked it away. Brandon was still breathing. There was blood welling up on both men in the chest area. I needed help now.

I turned and ran for the house, charging through the open gate, gun in hand. I didn't stop to wonder if the man had a wife or the yellow Lab would attack. I needed a phone and I needed it now.

No one in the backyard; the Lab woofed in a token way from a dog run. The sliding glass door at the back of the big house was half-open. I dashed across the deck and into the room and looked wildly around.

The room seemed vast and dark. I could see a TV and a table. The walls were covered with what looked like bulletin boards that were plastered in newspaper clippings. There was a desk with a computer in the corner. And next to the computer was a phone. I lunged desperately in that direction.

Dialing 911, I waited for the crisp, professional voice.

"Do you have an emergency?"

"I do. Two men have been shot. I need help," I said. And was very pleased to find I could speak at all.

Chapter 23

A WEEK LATER I WAS finally able to take a deep breath. Brandon Carter was alive and in the hospital. The doctors thought he would make it. The man who shot him, one Richard Brewster, was dead. By my hand. I still could not quite assimilate this.

Richard Brewster, who had run me off many years ago when I had ridden up to the back of his property on my horse, had apparently nurtured a hatred of equestrians along with a hugely territorial sense of his own space. He had also, apparently, been obsessed with various serial trailside killers—his walls were papered with newspaper and magazine accounts of these murders. His diary reflected what sounded like an insatiable urge to combine his vendetta against trail riders with his lust to become just such an infamous killer himself. For years he had practiced at the range with a long-barreled twenty-two pistol, working to become an expert sniper from a distance. His journals chronicled his goal of "picking off those damn women on their horses. They won't know what hit them."

By his own account, Richard Brewster hiked the trails with his dog in order to become an expert at where to lie in wait. He knew every hidden spot with a good line of sight. As he said, "I'm invisible with the stupid dog. Just another middle-aged dog walker. No one has any idea what I'm up to." He had purchased the Lab from a duck hunter who had guaranteed the dog had no fear of gunfire and knew how to lie down and stay still and quiet on command.

Jeri Ward had been able to give me the other facts I desperately needed. Richard Brewster was single, had never been married or had children. His parents were dead. I had taken nobody's husband or father or child. I had saved Brandon's life (I hoped) and rid the trails of the killer who haunted them. Jeri herself had adopted the big yellow Lab. And Trish O'Hara and Coal were just fine.

Sometimes when I lay awake at night I could see Richard Brewster lying there on the ground, as I had waited beside him and Brandon for the paramedics. I had known he wasn't breathing. But Brandon was. I was pretty sure I felt okay about this. I had not told Mac, however.

Since the day when I had called 911, it had rained almost nonstop. Great blasts of wind and rolls of thunder; a deluge pouring down. The streams all had running water in them. The ponds were filling. But after a week of blustery weather, the skies had cleared. Today was bright and warm and blue and smiling.

The storm was over, in more than one way. Sunshine poured over the ridge and filled my little hollow in the hills. Mac was playing with Star; Blue was working in the vegetable garden. As for me, I saddled Sunny. Brushing his woolly coat and combing his long mane, I glanced at the familiar ridgeline, seeing the landmark tree silhouetted against the sky. And I smiled.

"We're okay," I said softly, and with gratitude. "We're all okay. Thank you."

And I headed out to ride the trails along the ridge.

Epilogue

I THINK OF DEATH SOMETIMES, when I lie awake at night. I know that I, too, will die. I imagine that I will die in this bed. I try to guess what this will be like. Perhaps I will be an old woman, with my grown son at my bedside. Even then, I suppose, my thoughts will turn to him, to be sure he is all right without me. I see myself smiling at him, in reassurance. In my mind, Mac smiles back and holds my hand.

Somehow, in this fantasy, Blue is already dead, gone before me, and as I ready myself to let go of my body, I see Blue coming toward me through a field of grass, awash in light. Coming with him is a troop of creatures large and small—my beloved horses, dogs, cats and others, from chickens to a broken-legged sparrow I tried and failed to save, and a blind kitten that I rescued from under the hooves of a horse and had to euthanize. My heart fills with joy as I see them all, coming to greet me.

I smile, this time at Blue and my animals. Mac sees the smile and squeezes my hand gently, understanding that it's all okay.

"I love you," I say. To Mac, to Blue, to my animals, to the sweet world, to everything.

And I let go.

Shmuel Thaler

About the Author

Laura Crum (pictured with Sunny), a fourth-generation Santa Cruz County resident, has owned and trained horses for over thirty years. She lives and gardens in the hills near California's Monterey Bay with her husband, son, and a large menagerie of horses, dogs, cats, and chickens. She may be e-mailed and visited at www.lauracrum.com and www.equestrianink.blogspot.com.

MORE MYSTERIES
FROM PERSEVERANCE PRESS
🂠 *For the New Golden Age* 🂠

JON L. BREEN
Eye of God
ISBN 978-1-880284-89-6

TAFFY CANNON
ROXANNE PRESCOTT SERIES
Guns and Roses
Agatha and Macavity awards nominee, Best Novel
ISBN 978-1-880284-34-6

Blood Matters
ISBN 978-1-880284-86-5

Open Season on Lawyers
ISBN 978-1-880284-51-3

Paradise Lost
ISBN 978-1-880284-80-3

LAURA CRUM
GAIL MCCARTHY SERIES
Moonblind
ISBN 978-1-880284-90-2

Chasing Cans
ISBN 978-1-880284-94-0

Going, Gone
ISBN 978-1-880284-98-8

Barnstorming
ISBN 978-1-56474-508-8

JEANNE M. DAMS
HILDA JOHANSSON SERIES
Crimson Snow
ISBN 978-1-880284-79-7

Indigo Christmas
ISBN 978-1-880284-95-7

Murder in Burnt Orange
ISBN 978-1-56474-503-3

JANET DAWSON
JERI HOWARD SERIES
Bit Player
ISBN 978-1-56474-494-4

What You Wish For
(forthcoming)
ISBN 978-1-56474-518-7

KATHY LYNN EMERSON
LADY APPLETON SERIES
Face Down Below the Banqueting House
ISBN 978-1-880284-71-1

Face Down Beside St. Anne's Well
ISBN 978-1-880284-82-7

Face Down O'er the Border
ISBN 978-1-880284-91-9

ELAINE FLINN
MOLLY DOYLE SERIES
Deadly Vintage
ISBN 978-1-880284-87-2

SARA HOSKINSON FROMMER
JOAN SPENCER SERIES
Her Brother's Keeper
(forthcoming)
ISBN 978-1-56474-525-5

HAL GLATZER
KATY GREEN SERIES
Too Dead To Swing
ISBN 978-1-880284-53-7

A Fugue in Hell's Kitchen
ISBN 978-1-880284-70-4

The Last Full Measure
ISBN 978-1-880284-84-1

MARGARET GRACE
MINIATURE SERIES
Mix-up in Miniature
ISBN 978-1-56474-510-1

WENDY HORNSBY
MAGGIE MACGOWEN SERIES
In the Guise of Mercy
ISBN 978-1-56474-482-1

The Paramour's Daughter
ISBN 978-1-56474-496-8

The Hanging *(forthcoming)*
ISBN 978-1-56474-526-2

DIANA KILLIAN
POETIC DEATH SERIES
Docketful of Poesy
ISBN 978-1-880284-97-1